PASS CREEK VALLEY

Center Point
Large Print

Also by Wayne D. Overholser and available from Center Point Large Print:

Black Mike
The Durango Stage
Proud Journey
The Trouble Kid

**This Large Print Book carries the
Seal of Approval of N.A.V.H.**

PASS CREEK VALLEY

— A Western Duo —

Wayne D. Overholser

CENTER POINT LARGE PRINT
THORNDIKE, MAINE

This Center Point Large Print edition is published
in the year 2016 by arrangement with
Golden West Literary Agency.

The text of this Large Print edition is unabridged.
In other aspects, this book may vary from the original edition.
Printed in the United States of America on permanent paper.
Set in 16-point Times New Roman type.

ISBN: 978-1-68324-113-3 (hardcover)
ISBN: 978-1-68324-117-1 (softcover)

Library of Congress Cataloging-in-Publication Data

Names: Overholser, Wayne D., 1906–1996, author. | Overholser,
Wayne D., 1906–1996. Stage to Death. | Overholser, Wayne D.,
1906-1996. Pass Creek Valley.
Title: Pass Creek Valley : a western duo / Wayne D. Overholser.
Description: Center Point Large Print edition. | Thorndike, Maine :
Center Point Large Print, 2016.
Identifiers: LCCN 2016024188| ISBN 9781683241133 (hardcover :
alk. paper) | ISBN 9781683241171 (pbk. : alk. paper)
Subjects: LCSH: Large type books. | GSAFD: Western stories.
Classification: LCC PS3529.V33 A6 2016 | DDC 813/.54—dc23
LC record available at https://lccn.loc.gov/2016024188

Table of Contents

STAGE TO DEATH

I

It had rained hard for two days, hard enough to turn the Suntex County roads into greasy gumbo and bring the creeks and rivers boiling over their banks. It had stopped now, but the May sky was still as gray as a goose wing, and bore promise of another downpour.

Bill Mason, stage guard on the Opal City to Tamarack run, stood against the bar in the Last Chance Saloon, and stared thoughtfully through the fly-specked window at the leaden sky. In a few minutes the stage would pull out for Tamarack. Maybe it would get through and maybe it wouldn't, for it had to cross Sundown and Paiute Rivers, and both were mud-yellow, roaring torrents.

"Hello, Billy Bock," a man said softly.

Icy fingers knotted Bill's stomach muscles. He hadn't been called Billy Bock since he'd been a wild young hellion back in the Colorado mining camps. Here in Oregon nobody knew who he was. Nobody knew what he'd been. Nobody knew about the bank job in Silver Creek where he'd had his first and last taste of the Owlhoot, and found it not to his liking. He was Bill Mason, stage guard, with a three-year perfect record to his credit. Slowly Bill's eyes turned to the man who had come up behind him. He was a stranger clad in a yellow slicker, a leggy man almost as tall as Bill with a saber-like nose and a pair of eyes as hard and sharp as chipped obsidian. A tough hand, Bill saw, with the stamp of the Owlhoot upon him.

"You got me wrong, feller," Bill made himself say. "My handle's Mason. Bill Mason."

"Sure, I know." The man's voice was so low that his words barely reached Bill's ears. "You're Bill Mason now, all right. It wouldn't do to be Billy Bock out here. Some folks wouldn't like it if they found out the gent they looked up to on account of his guts and fast guns had committed a robbery back in Silver Creek, Colorado."

The icy fingers took another tie on the knot in Bill's stomach. He'd never seen the man before, but the man knew. There was no use arguing. Bill had drifted for years after the Silver Creek episode, trying to get away from his past and forget it. He thought he'd done that here in Opal City. Now suddenly he realized these three years had been a fool's paradise. For a moment he stared unseeingly at the amber liquid in the glass before him, a long moment while the past caught up with him and held him in its long and cruel tentacles.

"You seem to know quite a bit, feller," Bill said then.

"Yeah, quite a bit," the man murmured. "I ain't got nothing against you, Billy Bock. Neither's the Domino Kid."

Bill's eyes stabbed at the man. "I don't know

the Domino Kid. What's he got to do with it?"

"Plenty. You'd know the Kid all right if you seen him without his mask, but we'll let that go. What I'm getting at is whether you're gonna be smart so we can make a deal, or if you're gonna be fool enough to make me tell certain folks about the Silver Creek job."

"What's the deal?"

"In a few minutes you'll be heading out with Mack Travers. Your box is gonna be heavy, heavy enough to make good picking for the Kid. Now the Kid don't want no trouble. Of course, if there is trouble, I reckon he can handle it, and the way the weather is, he could get clear before the sheriff caught his trail. Still and all, the Kid don't like shooting. If you'd just hand the box down, and forget your guns, I'll ride on, and nobody's gonna know about Silver Creek."

Bill looked down at the glass again. "Maybe certain folks wouldn't believe your yarn."

"And again they might. Travers is no friend of yours. Neither is Eli Krone in Tamarack. Even Sam Benton might do a little quizzing around if he knew what I know."

All that was true enough. Both Travers and Krone, the Tamarack agent, were new men, and they'd plainly showed their dislike for Bill. Why, he didn't know, but he did know he valued Sam Benton's friendship and trust. Benton was the superintendent, and he'd given Bill his job. Then there was Laura Benton, Sam's girl. Six months ago she'd returned to Opal City from Portland where she'd been going to school. From the moment Bill had seen her standing beside Sam's desk, he'd known exactly what the future would be for him without Laura. Balancing that knowledge had been the bitter realization that a man with his past could never tell her how he felt.

"Well?" the man asked. "What's it going to be?"

Bill gulped his drink, and slid the glass back across the bar. "How'd you know so much about the set-up here?"

"That's none of your business. I'm asking one question and I want the answer."

Bill drew paper and tobacco from his pocket. His fingers trembled a little as he spilled the tobacco into the brown paper. There was only one answer he could make, and he knew the price he'd pay in making it. Sam Benton had trusted him. Benton hadn't asked him for his pedigree. There was only one way to return a trust like that.

"The answer is that you can go to hell," Bill said evenly as he shaped up his smoke.

The man grinned wolfishly. "I ain't surprised. It's sure funny how righteous a gent gets when he thinks he's got a good thing. You're a fool, Billy Bock. You rode with Stony Krass once. That put a brand on you you'll always wear. After you think about it a spell mebbe you'll get over being a fool. I ain't telling Benton now what I know. I'm giving you a chance. The Domino Kid is taking the box between here and Tamarack. If you go for your guns, Benton will hear the dirt. Think it over."

The man stepped around Bill, and strode out of the saloon. A moment later he rode by on a big roan gelding, headed west for Tamarack.

Bill laid a coin on the bar.

"Better have another drink," the apron said as he came up. "It'll be a hard trip to Tamarack today."

"That it will," Bill agreed. "No, one's enough."

"I hear the Paiute and Sundown are running chockfull. If them bridges go out, you'll be stuck on the peninsula. Looks to me like Sam's a fool to send you out."

Bill shrugged. "The mail has to go through. I reckon the bridges will be there long enough for us to get over 'em."

The stage was standing in front of the office when Bill reached it. Mack Travers scowled. "I didn't look for you to show up. I figured maybe you were too yellow to make the trip today."

Bill's fists knotted. "Mack, one of these days you're going to waggle that long tongue of yours too much. I don't like sitting beside you any more than you do me, but there isn't any sense in acting like a mangy hound with a sore tail even if you are one."

Travers's beefy face reddened with anger. He started to say something, and didn't, for Sam

Benton appeared in the doorway behind Bill. He called: "Bill, come in here a minute!"

Bill felt the icy fingers working his stomach muscles again. Maybe the sharp-nosed stranger had told him already.

Benton was pacing the length of the office when Bill went in. He was a white-haired, steady-eyed oldster who had done just about everything for Wells, Fargo in the years he'd been with them. He stopped pacing now, and looked at Bill worriedly.

"It's gonna be a hell of a trip," Benton said bluntly. "The road's slick and the bridges may go out any time. What's more, you've got a heavy box. You'll have the mine payroll, and a sack of gold for the Tamarack bank. To make it worse, you've got four passengers, one of 'em Laura."

"Laura?" Bill stared at the superintendent in amazement. "What are you letting her go for?"

"I don't tell Laura what she can or can't do," Benton snapped. "She's twenty-one, and she knows how things are as well as I do. Besides, she's told folks she's going, and there'd be a row if I tried to keep her from it." He looked at Bill narrowly. "I was thinking maybe you wouldn't want to go today."

Bill couldn't tell, as he met Benton's gaze, whether the sharp-nosed man had stopped and told Benton or not. He asked quietly: "Are you telling me I'm fired, Sam?"

"No," Benton answered. "You've got the best

record of any guard I've got. I just thought maybe you wouldn't want to go today."

"I heard a yarn about the Domino Kid being between here and Tamarack," Bill said, and saw the superintendent's face whiten.

"That heller?" Benton rumbled. "I don't believe it. The last thing I heard he was clear over on Snake River."

"Just a rumor," Bill said mildly. "A gent in the Last Chance was telling me about it. If you aren't firing me, I'm going. I figure I'd do as well handling the Kid as anybody. But there's one thing, Sam. I'm not riding with Travers after this trip."

Sam Benton nodded somberly. "He's an ornery cuss all right, and he isn't too smart about some things, but he's a steady enough driver. He'll get the stage through if anybody can."

Laura Benton came in then from the street. She looked prettier than ever, Bill thought, in her plum-colored taffeta dress and the bright blue bonnet that matched her eyes. Again that chill spasm hit his stomach, for the past was rushing up once more, dispelling the bright promise that her presence always held for him, a promise that could never be borne out.

"You shouldn't be going today," Bill said roughly. "It's a dangerous trip. There's nothing in Tamarack that warrants taking the risk."

"That's what a man would say." Laura's full, red lips smiled at him, but there was that in her eyes

15

telling Bill he could say nothing to change her mind. "With Mack Travers driving, and you riding shotgun, I'm taking no risk. My best friend is getting married in Tamarack tomorrow, Bill. I wouldn't miss it for anything."

"You see?" Sam spread his hands helplessly. "She'll go. Hell or high water wouldn't stop her."

Bill said nothing more. He helped Travers carry the heavy box to the stage and slide it under the seat. Laura stepped inside. Bill climbed to the seat beside Travers, and they rolled down the muddy street to the hotel. Three passengers got in there. One was Joe Higgins, a bleary-eyed whiskey drummer, the second a sheepman from Tamarack named Hank Fletcher. The third Bill didn't know. He was a slim, dapper man in a black broadcloth suit. He wore two guns on his lean hips, and there was a sort of feline toughness about him that Bill noted.

Later, when the town was behind them, and they were wheeling through the sticky gumbo, Bill asked: "Who's the dude?"

"Dunno." Travers spat over the wheel. "Stranger in town." He looked at Bill and grinned sourly. "You worried, Mason? Think maybe we got the Domino Kid with us?"

"Maybe." Bill looked at the driver narrowly. "How come you think he's in these parts?"

Travers shrugged his thick shoulders. "You never know where that hellion's gonna be. I'd heard he was around. That's why I figured you wouldn't be going today. I reckon he's one *hombre* you wouldn't care to swap lead with."

Bill kept a tight rein on his temper. That was Travers clean through. He'd go out of his way to make a man mad for no reason.

For an hour they rode in silence under a lowering sky. Carefully Bill went over in his mind the route between Opal City and Tamarack, picking out the spots where the Domino Kid might set his trap. It wouldn't be on the flat between Opal City and Sundown Cañon, nor would it likely be between the Paiute west rim and Tamarack. There were two sharp grades down to the rivers, and two hard climbs above them. The chances were the Kid would strike near the top of one of the climbs.

No one seemed to know anything about the Domino Kid except that he wore a black and white checked mask—that he was deadly with six-guns. There was no description of his looks because no one had ever seen his face when he was holding up a stage, but he'd just about match the dude in the coach in size. He usually worked with two men. Bill had never heard of him operating in Oregon, but the outlaw had found it too hot in Montana and Wyoming where he had been working. There was a good chance the Domino Kid had moved west.

Bill thought again about Stony Krass, the outlaw

with whom he had ridden when they'd held up the Silver Creek Bank. Bill had heard he'd been shot a year or so after that, but someone in Krass's crowd must have spotted Bill Mason as the Billy Bock of the Colorado mining camps. Otherwise, the sharp-nosed stranger would never have known who he was.

They started down the steep grade to Sundown River, slithering perilously close to the edge as they swung around the curves. Bill held his shotgun between his legs, eyes on the road below, but it was from habit more than any thought the Domino Kid would be here. He was thinking about the stranger, about Laura Benton, and he wondered bitterly why life had brought them together after it was too late.

Then they'd reached the bottom, and swung south along the riverbank. A quarter of a mile upstream was the bridge, the muddy, yellow torrent sweeping fiercely under it. A mass of logs and débris was jammed against the pier, and it seemed to Bill that the bridge was about ready to go.

"It doesn't look good, Travers," he said. "You'd better let the passengers out before you . . ."

"You're yellow," Travers snarled. "Yellow like that damned soup. Hang on. I'll get you over. Or maybe you want to get down."

"Go ahead," Bill said through tight lips. "We'll all get wet together." It seemed to him, as it had more than once before, that the driver was trying to prod him into making some loco move. He didn't understand why, but he kept a tight rein on his temper. There would come a time for settlement with Travers.

The stage swung west, rumbling on across the swaying bridge, and reached the west side. Travers leered at Bill.

"I reckon you'd've had us sitting all night waiting for the water to go down. There isn't no room for a yellow-bellied jigger in this business."

Bill's fists clenched. "Travers, I'm a mite tired of hearing that kind of gab. When we get to Tamarack, I'm gonna shove it down your throat."

"Yeah, sure," Travers mocked. "You'll play . . ."

A timber-splintering crash came from behind them as the river triumphed, and swept the span downstream. Travers whipped a glance behind them, and what he saw brought a strained look into his beefy face.

"Sure," Bill jeered, "you'd've had us all taking a cold bath, and heading downstream for the Columbia."

For once Travers was silent. The road tilted sharply now, bringing the horses to a slow, slogging pace. This was where Bill had guessed the Domino Kid would be. Bill gripped his shotgun, eyes hard on the narrow road above, nerves taut as his gaze searched every boulder and break in the steep walls ahead.

Slowly they crawled up the gash of a road as

gray clouds dropped lower. Then they were on top and leveling out across the summit. The road swung south again. They were across the divide, and starting down the grade to the Paiute. It twisted a thousand feet below them, running as yellow and fiercely as the Sundown. The bridge across it was much like the one that had gone out behind them. Bill wondered what Travers would do when he reached it.

The coach swayed ponderously down the grade, sliding close to the edge and back again as the straining driver gripped the brake handle and called to the horses. A grim look came to Bill Mason's lean face as he considered the possibility of the bridge below them being out. They'd be marooned here on the peninsula between the rivers, for days perhaps, without food and without water. Bill thought of the Domino Kid, and he thought of Laura Benton in the coach, and he swore softly.

Then they were down, and rolling upstream alongside the river. The bridge was still in place. There was no log jam against it, but muddy water was running over the plank floor. Fifty yards or more above the bridge was a homesteader's deserted shack and barn. Travers didn't make the turn toward the bridge, but tooled the coach off the road, and across the meadow to the barn. Bill looked at Travers sharply, but the driver kept his eyes straight ahead, his mouth a hard line across his red face.

When the horses stopped beside the barn, Hank Fletcher poked his head out, and yelled: "Hey, you mule-headed numbskull, what are you doing here?"

Travers climbed down. "Maybe you want to take a swim, Fletcher, but I don't. We're staying here tonight."

"What the hell," the sheep rancher bawled. "I've got to be in Tamarack tonight."

"Walking's good," Travers said laconically. "We just missed getting our feet wet when we crossed the Sundown. I can't tell what shape this bridge is in, but I'm not taking any chances. We'll stay here tonight. It isn't cold, and it isn't raining. You'll be all right. Come morning, if the water's down, we'll go on."

Fletcher started to curse again. Bill had come up behind Travers, his shotgun in his hand. He said: "Shut up, sheepherder, or I'll pull you out of there, and throw you into the Paiute."

The sheepman subsided. Bill wheeled, and went into the barn. The roof of the house had fallen in, but the barn was in fair shape. If it rained during the night, they might get wet, but it was better than sleeping in the mud. He left the barn, and walked to the bridge. For a time he stood looking at it, wondering why Travers had decided not to cross it. It didn't add up right. But Bill figured he'd know the answer before daylight.

II

Travers was unhitching the horses when Bill came up. "You open your mug about me being scared of crossing the Paiute, and I'll pull it out of your head, Mason," the driver snarled.

"I wouldn't think of it, Mack. I don't need to say anything."

"It was just the smart thing to do," Travers muttered. "No use taking chances."

"Sure, and we'll be handy for the Domino Kid if he is holing up around here."

"That's your job," he said sullenly.

"Yeah," Bill agreed. "That's my job. I aim to make it tough for the Kid, and anybody that's aiding him."

"Keep an eye on that gun-packing dude," Travers muttered, and turned back to his horses.

The passengers were huddled in the barn. Laura looked at Bill, and challenged him with a smile. "I guess you're still thinking I shouldn't have come."

"When's the wedding?" Bill asked.

"Tomorrow afternoon," Laura answered.

"Maybe you'll make it yet."

Bill explored the barn. Stalls ran along one half of the north side. The other half was a large, rectangular pen. The floor of the south end was covered with musty straw. He went back to the passengers. "I'll see if we can rustle an axe. We can chance a fire here in the pen. It'll be mighty cold by morning if we don't have one."

The dude's brows lifted. "I'd rather be cold than have our hotel burn up," he said sourly.

"It won't burn," Bill said, and left the barn.

Bill searched the shack. In a lean-to behind it, he found a rusty axe. He split some dry wood he found in the lean-to, and carried it to the barn.

Joe Higgins, the whiskey drummer, had opened his bag and was sampling a bottle. Bill dropped the wood, jerked the bottle from Higgins's mouth, and tossed it into the straw. Higgins spluttered an oath, and swung his right fist at Bill.

"Behave," Bill snapped, and caught the drummer's fist, but Higgins was in no mood to behave. He slashed his left fist into Bill's face, tried to twist free, and failed. It wasn't a hard blow, but it was enough to snap the last shred of Bill's temper. He jerked the drummer toward him, stooped, and in a continuation of the same lightning movement he raised his shoulder into the man's middle, and pinwheeled the drummer through the air behind him. Higgins smashed into the wall, bounced off, and hit the earth floor in a wind-driving fall.

Travers had been standing in the runway at the end of the barn, watching Bill. Now he let out a bellow of rage, his red face contorted by a swift rush of fury.

"You can't throw my passengers around!" Travers roared, and started toward Bill. "Shuck off your gun belts, and we'll see who's running this outfit."

"Suits me," Bill rasped. He unbuckled his gun belts and handed them to Laura. "Come on, Mack. You've been wanting this for a long time."

Travers came in a rush, big fists flying. Bill was lighter than Travers, but faster. He pivoted lightly to one side, clipped Travers hard on the side of the head, and sent him spinning into the wall. Travers smashed against the boards, spun away, and came rushing. This time Bill met him with an impact that jarred the building. Bill's fists beat viciously into the driver's thick-muscled stomach, battered his head back with short, trip-hammer punches, and drove him into a corner. Travers plunged to one side and backed away.

Bill kept after Travers, never letting him get set for a solid counterpunch. Travers was bleeding from mouth and nose, and his eyes were beginning to close. He drove a few blows home, but Bill kept him enough off balance so that his fists did little more than sting Bill's face. They made a complete circle, Bill stalking as a cougar might stalk his prey.

"Come on and fight," Bill taunted. "You've been calling the wrong man yellow, Travers."

Travers held his ground then, great fists sweeping at Bill's face. One of them landed, the

24

first effective blow the driver had smashed home. Fireworks exploded before Bill's eyes. He took a battering fist on his shoulder, blocked another with his arms, and, when his vision had cleared, he drove in hard. Travers didn't back up in time. Bill rocked the driver's head with a pile-driving right, and he heard Laura cry out. Once more Bill's fist cracked against Travers's jaw. The driver started to go down, great arms sagging. As he fell, Bill hit him with all his hundred and eighty pounds of hard muscle behind the blow. Travers fell soddenly into the ancient litter of the stable floor, and lay still.

Bill sleeved sweat from his forehead. As he took the gun belts from Laura, he saw that she was staring steadily at Travers's still body. Then she raised her eyes to Bill's. "Did you have to do that?"

Bill laughed harshly. "What did you want me to do?" He buckled on the belts, and began to build a fire in the center of the pen. The gun-slung dude came up to him.

"Queer business," he said. "What's behind it?"

Bill straightened up. The whiskey drummer, Higgins, was on his feet now, and Fletcher was eyeing him curiously.

"I'm just not sure," Bill said. "I've got it pretty straight that the Domino Kid is around here, expecting to grab that express box. I haven't figured out why Travers didn't cross the bridge.

Maybe he knows more than I do, but it doesn't look to me like the bridge over the Paiute is half as dangerous to travel as the one we did cross."

"We beat that one by seconds," the dude said thoughtfully, "but I didn't think it looked quite right when he turned off here."

"I'm guessing the Kid was somewhere on the road beyond the Paiute," Bill went on. "Maybe just below the rim. It's steep right there, and we'd have been moving slow. I figure we're as well off here as we could have been if the Kid had tackled us below the rim. That's why you aren't taking on a skin full of your forty-rod, Higgins. Before the night's over, we may need all the guns we've got." Travers had come around now, his hate-filled eyes on Bill. "From here on in I'm running things. You hear that, Travers?" The driver nodded sullenly, and made no move to get up. "You, Higgins?" The whiskey drummer bobbed his head. "All right. Some of you will get some sleep. Laura, we can fix you a bed over there in the straw. The rest of us will stay here. If we aren't lucky, we'll be stopping lead by morning."

For a time none of them said anything. They stood looking at Bill until the gun-packing dude said: "I've heard of the Domino Kid. If he is around, we'll be lucky if we don't all stop some lead."

Travers got up and lurched out of the barn. Bill nodded at Higgins and Fletcher. "Go over to the lean-to and get some wood," he ordered. When they were gone, Bill said: "It's gonna be tough sledding here tonight. I'm not sure of Travers. If he's thrown in with the Kid, he may get the drop on us."

There was a bleak smile on the dude's face. "Could be you're suspicious of me, too. I hope you'll believe me. I'm Brad Buckley. I'd heard the Tamarack Bar was for sale. I'm going over to see about it." He lowered his voice. "I'm packing a nice chunk of *dinero*. I might just as well stop some of the Kid's lead if I lose it."

"You look like you might be some help when the shooting starts," Bill said. "Higgins won't, and Fletcher's the kind that's likely to start things at the wrong time." He looked at Laura, and slowly shook his head. "Lady, I'm sure sorry you're here."

"I'm not." There was no fear in her blue eyes when she looked up at Bill. "I wouldn't miss this for the world."

Bill groaned. "I suppose you think it'll be as much fun as a wedding."

"Certainly, and a lot more exciting."

Bill threw up his hands. "All right. Just stick around. You'll have your excitement. Buckley, when I'm not here, I want you to stay here with Laura. She might be as profitable for the Kid as the express box."

III

It was dusk when Bill left the barn and walked to the coach. A few minutes later he came back with the express box, and dropped it outside the pen in the straw. Fletcher and Higgins were standing beside Buckley at the fire. Neither Laura nor Travers was in sight.

"Where's Laura?" Bill demanded.

Buckley looked around in surprise. "I dunno. Thought she was in here."

Bill swore. "Where's Travers?"

"He hasn't been here since he got up after his licking," Buckley answered.

Bill wheeled out of the barn. It had begun to rain again, not heavily, but enough to make a person wet, and Laura was out in it. He circled the barn, searched the house, and finally found her standing beside the bridge.

"What are you doing here?"

"Getting rained on," she said flippantly. "If you don't get me to that wedding, Bill Mason, I'll never speak to you again."

"All I want is to get you out of here alive," Bill snapped. "After this you stay in the barn. Did you see Travers?"

"Bill"—she grabbed his arm, the flippancy gone

28

from her voice now—"Travers is over there on the other side of the river. Why would he be there?"

"My guess is he's expecting to find the Domino Kid. Come on. You're getting back to the barn. When the blow-off comes, you get down behind a manger and stay there."

"Yes," Laura said meekly, and walked back to the barn, her arm through Bill's.

For one short moment Bill dreamed a dream that had been with him from the time he'd first seen Laura. Then, like all dreams, it was gone, for the past had rushed up again. Silver Creek. Stony Krass. The sharp-nosed stranger. Billy Bock, the bank robber.

"What are you thinking, Bill?" Laura asked.

Bill looked down at her, and he thought bitterly he could never tell her what he had really been thinking. He said: "I was thinking about how to keep you out of the Domino Kid's hands. He may get the idea your dad would dig deep into his pocket to get you back with your hide all in one piece."

For a long time they sat around the fire while darkness came and the rain pounded against the roof. "What do you figure about Travers?" Buckley asked suddenly.

"If he comes in, don't take any chances." Bill took off his slicker. "In the dark and that rain, the Domino Kid and an army could sneak up on us.

One of us has got to stay outside. Who wants the first crack at it?"

Hank Fletcher pulled at the ends of his scraggly mustache. "Reckon it might as well be me."

"Fire a shot if you need any help," Bill said, "and keep fairly close to the barn. Come in every half hour or so."

"Sure," Fletcher said. He slipped into the slicker, and went out.

Bill picked up Higgins's coat. "Come on, Laura. You're going to bed." He laid the coat on the straw on the other side of the row of mangers but, when he came back, Laura hadn't stirred.

"I'm not sleepy," she said defiantly.

"All right," Bill said. "Get in the way if you want to."

They sat around the fire, talking little. Higgins kept licking his lips, and looking at his bag. Buckley stared somberly into the fire. Bill moved to the door occasionally, and looked out into the rainy night, Laura's eyes following him where she sat across the fire from Buckley. Once she got up and moved to him.

"Did you see Fletcher?" she asked.

"No." Bill answered. "I'm going out and look." He stepped out of the barn. Five minutes he was back. He hesitated a moment, eyes on Laura. "You might as well know. Fletcher's out there by the coach, dead. He's been knifed."

For the first time real fear came into Laura

Benton's blue eyes. She clutched Bill's arm. "The Domino Kid?" she asked.

Bill nodded somberly. "I'd never heard he was a knifer. Gunslingers don't usually have any need for knives." He'd been holding a hand behind his back. Now he brought it around him, and showed Laura the bloody, long-bladed knife he held. The handle showed a black and white checked design. "That was in Fletcher's chest. Reckon it's the Domino Kid's all right."

Buckley was standing across the fire from Bill, staring at Bill's face rather than the knife. Joe Higgins was still crouched by the fire, whiskey-bleared eyes wide with fear, the smell of liquor about him.

"Damn you, Higgins!" Bill roared. "You've been into your bag again. How can you do any straight shooting if you're gonna fill your hide with your rotten whiskey?"

Higgins licked his lips. "I just had a snort," he whined. "I ain't got a gun anyway."

"Buckley's got two," Bill snapped. "When they rush us, you'll need . . ."

Buckley had stepped away from the fire, and for the moment Bill's eyes had not been on him. In that moment his hand darted down, and plucked a gun. Laura cried out.

"Take it easy." Buckley was grinning broadly, his eyes on Bill. "The Domino Kid plays it a little different this time, *hombre*. He rides along

31

nice and comfortable in the stage, holes up with you when Travers gets scared of the bridge, and now he rakes in the pot. I've heard how fast you are with your guns, Mason. I figured this would be the easiest way since you didn't want to play smart, and tell Poke you'd sit tight."

Bill could curse himself for a fool. The Domino Kid had played him for a sucker. He'd been suspicious of the dude at first, and then he'd believed his story about going to Tamarack to buy the saloon.

Laura's fingers tightened on Bill's arm. "You're the Domino Kid?" she asked. "You couldn't have knifed Fletcher."

Buckley laughed softly. "I'm the Domino Kid, all right, and I knew this was the time to hit the stage. Your smart gun guard there gave me another idea. I'll take you along. It might just be your dad thinks enough of you to pay. No, I didn't knife Fletcher. I've got a couple of good men out there." He whistled. A moment later Travers and the sharp-nosed man came in. "You got the horses, Poke?"

The sharp-nosed man nodded. "Mine and yours, and one for Travers."

"Good." Buckley nodded, his eyes not leaving Bill's face. "Harness up the horses, Travers. We're taking the stage. I figure somebody'll be out tomorrow finding out why the stage didn't get in, and they might be suspicious if they see it. Did you gents go through the mail bags?"

"Nothing there," Travers said. "We was at it when Fletcher showed up. That's why we had to beef him."

"Get at the horses, Travers," Buckley ordered. "Poke, the box is over there. Put it on the stage."

Bill tensed. He'd been waiting for a break, and it hadn't come. Buckley had expected him to make a try for his guns. Even a killer like the Domino Kid wanted an excuse to kill a man.

Buckley couldn't turn down the temptation to do some bragging. "I've never failed on a job," he said. "The reason I've never failed is because I don't tackle one that hasn't been thoroughly planned. After Travers caught on here, he kept me informed. Then when he recognized Eli Krone, he brought him in, and we were set. I reckon we might even pull another job or two before Sam gets wise. That's what was wrong with Stony Krass, Billy Bock. He just rode blind, and started shooting. Men like that don't last long. You've got to work at this same as anything else."

Poke had carried the box back to the coach. Travers led the horses outside, and Poke came back in.

"All set, Kid," Poke said.

But Buckley was enjoying himself too much to go yet. He drew a black and white checked hood from his pocket, and tossed it at Bill's feet. "That's my brand, gun guard. I'll leave it here with your carcass so the sheriff'll know who pulled the job. I always believe in advertising. It's easier when you keep folks scared." He nodded at Laura. "You get in the stage. Your friend, Mason here, will be kind of messed up when I get done. I'm right sorry about this, Mason. From all I hear, you've been a good guard, but good guards make my business tough."

"Hold on," Bill said. The only thing he could do was to play for time, and hope that something would break. "Was this all planned with Travers?"

"Sure," Buckley said, his tone faintly mocking. "We didn't plan on the Sundown bridge going out like it did, but it made it reasonable when Travers pulled in here. That was a chunk of luck for us."

"From what I've heard of the Domino Kid," Bill said, "he was the kind of gent who'd give a man a chance with his gun. You act like you're gonna smoke me down cold."

"I let you keep your guns thinking the tough Bill Mason might make a play"—Buckley sneered, his cat-bright eyes never wavering from Bill's face—"but, hell, you haven't even tried, so I'll have to do it this way."

"How come you knew about the Silver Creek job," Bill asked, "and Stony Krass?"

"That was Eli Krone." Buckley laughed softly. "This is a hell of a way for a gun guard to die, but it'll have to do." Buckley thumbed back the hammer of his gun. "Poke, get this gal out of here. She don't seem to be able to go by herself."

IV

Then the whole thing broke, and in a way Bill hadn't expected. Nobody had been watching Joe Higgins. The whiskey drummer was still hunkered by the fire, but it had finally dawned on his liquor-fogged brain that, if Bill died, he'd die, too. He'd crept toward Buckley, and the outlaw didn't see him until he'd wrapped his arms around Buckley's legs. Poke apparently hadn't seen the whiskey drummer moving, either, for he'd been moving toward Laura.

Bill wheeled away from the fire, grabbing a gun as he moved. Buckley fired pointblank at Higgins. Poke, too, clawed for his gun, but he was far too slow. Bill pitched his first shot at Poke, and whirled toward Buckley just as the outlaw kicked himself free from Higgins's relaxed grip. Buckley swept his gun up toward Bill, but he'd lost a valuable second, a second long enough for Bill to line his gun on Buckley and squeeze the trigger. Buckley lurched with the impact of the slug, fired wildly once, and sprawled headlong toward the fire.

Poke was dead. Bill saw that, and he saw that his second bullet had ended the career of the Domino Kid, but Mack Travers was outside on the stage seat. Bill raced for the barn door. Travers already had the coach moving. He saw Bill come out, and curled his blacksnake over the horses' heads, the report of it mingling with the roar of Bill's gun. Bill fired again, and missed. Then the big coach was rumbling toward the bridge. Bill raced after it, but there was no catching up with it now.

Bill stopped, gun held high, but he held his fire. The gold was in the stagecoach, but the chances were good Mack Travers would never find out where. Besides, he'd likely go on to Tamarack and meet Eli Krone. Bill pictured the Tamarack agent's bearded face, tried to place him, and failed. He had no proof now against the agent except what the Domino Kid had said, but if Travers went on to Tamarack, Bill Mason would get the proof he needed.

When Bill got back to the barn, he found Laura bending over Bill Higgins. The whiskey drummer's shirt was soaked with blood, but he was alive. Laura had torn a piece off her underskirt, and bound the wound. Bill examined it, Higgins watching him worriedly.

"You're hit bad enough so that you can't ride a horse," Bill said, "but looks to me like you'll make it all right if you lie still. Laura and me will head for Tamarack. We'll send a doc back. There's enough wood here for you to keep the fire going till morning. The sky's clearing up. I reckon the rain's over, and tomorrow will be warmer." Bill stood up, and looked down at the wounded man. "Joe, you did a mighty brave thing. We'd both be dead by now if you hadn't taken a hand."

Higgins's white-lipped mouth shaped into a small grin. He whispered: "I knew that, Bill. The heller figured I was so no-account he didn't have to watch me. All he bothered to do was to keep his eyes on you. Say, throw the carcasses out, will you, Bill? They make plumb unpleasant company."

Bill dragged the bodies out of the barn, and threw Higgins's coat over him. Then he said: "We'll get you to Tamarack in time for that wedding, Laura. Let's ride. I don't know what these horses are like, but we'll find out."

Laura faced Bill, and for the first time since he'd known her, she seemed at a loss for something to say. "Bill, I . . . I, well, I guess you were right," she said contritely. "I had no business coming today."

"It's a little late now to think about that." Bill grinned at her. "Let's travel."

Bill could have caught the stage before it reached Tamarack, but he wanted to catch Eli Krone red-handed. His career as a gun guard was over. It was a fact he must face now, just as he had faced the fact that he could never tell Laura

Benton how he felt about her. She knew now who he was, what he had been. As she rode beside him through the rain, across the bridge, and on up the long grade to the west rim, she said nothing about it, but she'd heard the Domino Kid, and the outlaw had said enough.

There was just one more thing Bill Mason could do for Sam Benton before he left the country. That was to prove to him the part Eli Krone had had in the Domino Kid's sinister scheme. It was seldom Benton made a mistake in a man, and he hated to admit it when he did. He'd have to be shown hard, solid proof. So Bill and Laura stayed behind the stage after it reached the flat between the rim and Tamarack. The moon broke through the clouds.

When they were within a mile of Tamarack, Bill said: "I'm going on ahead, Laura. You follow along behind like we've been doing so you'll know if Travers stops or pulls off. If he does, you circle, and hightail it into town and find me. I'll be somewhere around the office."

"What are you going to do, Bill?"

"I aim to get the deadwood on Eli Krone," Bill said. "I'll get ahead of Travers, and be in Tamarack when he drives up. Chances are Krone will be in his office, waiting to make the split with Travers and the Domino Kid. You follow him in, but don't let him see you. Your dad keeps a room in the hotel. You go to it."

Bill left her then. He made a wide circle around

Travers, keeping a low ridge between him and the coach. It was nearly dawn when Bill rode into Tamarack, and the moon was again smothered behind thick clouds. There was a light in the express office window. Aside from that the town appeared lifeless.

Bill rode to the rear of the office, and left his horse behind it. He crouched in the alley beside the building, aware of voices from its interior. He couldn't make out what was being said, but one of the men was Sam Benton. The other was Eli Krone. With hard riding Benton could have reached Tamarack from Opal City by going south and crossing the upper bridges. Likely he had heard the lower bridge across the Sundown had gone out, and he had come on to see if the stage had reached Tamarack.

Then Bill heard the rumble of the coach. Krone and Benton must have heard it, too, for they came out and stood on the porch. The coach appeared out of the darkness. Krone said harshly: "You see, Sam. Mason isn't there. I'm betting Mack saved the gold for you." Even before the coach stopped rolling, Krone shouted: "What the hell happened, Mack?"

Travers pulled his horses to a stop. "Plenty. The Domino Kid was laying for us at the Paiute bridge. Mason was in with him, but I got both of 'em."

"Is Laura all right?" Benton asked.

"I reckon," Travers answered as he threw down the box. "The passengers are all in that barn above the bridge. I had to get on as fast as I could. They had a slick trap fixed up, but I got 'em."

Travers was on the ground now. He and Krone picked up the box, and carried it inside. Coldrage poured through Bill Mason then. Sam Benton was cursing Travers for leaving his daughter behind. The thing didn't make sense, and in a minute Sam would see it. Travers couldn't afford to wait long. He knew Bill was behind them. They'd kill Sam Benton, and open the express box. Softly Bill stepped around the corner, and crossed the porch. He passed a window just as Eli Krone was slashing down at Benton's head with a gun barrel. He'd waited too long, Bill thought desperately as he palmed a gun, went into the room.

Travers had the box open, his back to the door, and was cursing bitterly. "Rocks, Eli. Look! That damned Mason ran a sandy on us."

Then Krone saw Bill in the doorway, a bearded, bald-headed man, utter amazement mirrored in his pale eyes. Instantly his gun came up, and spat its tongue of orange flame at Bill. Lead splintered the doorjamb. That was the last shot Eli Krone fired, for Bill Mason's gun was bucking in his palm. He'd squeezed his trigger a split second before the agent had. Krone spilled forward over a chair, and onto the floor. Mack Travers had spun away from the table, and around, plucking his gun

40

as he turned. For this short interval it seemed to Bill Mason that time was flowing strongly against him. Travers had the first shot, and he didn't miss. There was the numbing impact of a slug ripping into Bill's left shoulder. He lurched with the slap of it, fired, and missed, and Travers, hurrying his second shot, missed, too.

Bill steadied then. Time was on his side now. It was enough. This time he didn't miss. Once, twice Bill's hammer dropped in a cold and merciless rhythm. Travers fell. In a sort of dogged determination Travers fought to his knees, hand groping blindly for his gun. He found it, raised it from the floor, but there was not the strength in his great body to prong back the hammer. He fell forward on his face, dead.

Outside there was the hoof pound of Laura's horse. Lights flamed to life along Tamarack's main street as gunfire broke into men's sleep, and brought them scurrying out of their rooms. A moment later Doc Bevins was in the office, hair rumpled, his black bag in his hand. An hour after that the crowd was gone, and a buckboard had been sent to Paiute bridge for Joe Higgins. Sam Benton had nothing more than a headache, but Bill Mason's bullet-ripped shoulder would be a long time mending.

Benton sat at the table in the office facing Bill, Laura beside him. She didn't smile when Bill said: "It's morning, Laura. You'd better go get some

41

sleep if you're going to look pretty for the wedding."

"That's not the wedding that counts," Laura said.

Bill looked at her, and for a moment he was stunned by the implication of her words.

Sam Benton chuckled softly. "It's quite a girl I've got, Bill. She's like a good horse. Needs a tight rein, but she'll go a long ways with the right man."

The right man! Bill stood up. "I guess I'm done in these parts," he said hoarsely. "I'll be riding on to some place they don't know I used to be called Billy Bock."

"You'll be riding nowhere," Benton snapped. "Don't be a fool. Sit down. I've suspicioned about you for a long time, but it makes no never mind to me. A man's past is his past. It's the present and the future I'm thinking about."

Bill sat down, his face showing his surprise. "You knew?"

"Well, I had an idea. I got a letter quite a spell ago from Tamarack signed 'Friend' by some jayhoo who didn't have guts enough to put his own handle down. I reckon it must've been Krone. The letter said you'd been with Stony Krass when the Silver Creek Bank had been held up. I wrote to Silver Creek, and the sheriff wrote back they didn't have no count against any Billy Bock. Stony Krass was dead, and the money had

42

been recovered. They didn't know who all was in the outfit, but the case was closed as far as they were concerned."

"If you knew . . . ?"

Benton held up his hand. "Of course I didn't really know. I figured somebody was trying to get rid of my best gun guard. Hell, man, you'd had plenty of chance to sell me out, and you hadn't. Yesterday that sharp-nosed stranger who was in Opal City came in, and gave me another yarn about you being an owlhooter. That was why I thought maybe you wouldn't want to make this run. I figured that, if you really had anything to be afraid of, you'd want to drift, but you didn't. Now that I've got the yarn about what happened at the bridge, I'll go so far as to promise you a job as long you want it."

"This Krone," Bill said thoughtfully. "The Domino Kid said he knew me, but I can't place him."

"He was giving me a big talk before the stage showed up about how he'd lived in Silver Creek, and he saw you holding the horses for Stony Krass's bunch when they knocked the bank over. I've heard him say he used to have a head of black hair. Now that he's bald-headed and raised a beard, I reckon he's changed."

Bill remembered then, a new man named York Logan who'd joined the outfit shortly before the Silver Creek hold-up. Logan, without the hair and

43

with the heavy beard, must and could have been Eli Krone.

"It was a slick trick all around," Benton went on, "just like one of the Domino Kid's jobs, only it backfired on him when that Poke *hombre* couldn't work you. I reckon Travers and Krone wouldn't have found the gold easily after you put it into one of Laura's bags."

"Only Laura maybe won't have the clothes she figured on wearing to the wedding," Bill said.

"It doesn't matter," Laura murmured. "I told you that it wasn't the wedding that mattered." She was coming toward Bill, her eyes on him, trying to tell him, just as her father had said, that the past is past, and the future is the only part of life that counts. Bill smiled a little then, and put his good right arm around her. It was the future he could see now, running its clear and promising trail ahead of him through the years, a trail that held a promise of reality for the dreams he'd dreamed. It looked to Bill, the way Laura was raising her face to his, that she was seeing the same long trail.

PASS CREEK
VALLEY

I

Kim Logan followed the pass road to the top until he saw the coach and six climbing far below him, then went on. No hurry. This might be a wild-goose chase, but still the job had to be thought out. That was a rule of the profession. The odds weren't so important if you had the edge and held it. Never pull a gun until you had to, and not then unless you're willing to kill. Never let the idea that the other man might be faster enter your mind.

Professor Kim Logan, M.G., Master of Guncraft. Kim laughed softly as he jogged down the slope. Why, he could write a book on how to be a tough hand. He had served his apprentice-ship on the border with as salty a crew as a man would find. The fact that he was alive at the ripe old age of twenty-five proved his fitness to write the book. He was the only one of the old bunch who could do any writing; the graves of the others were scattered from the Río Grande to the Dakota Badlands.

The summit was above timber line. Kim came to the first stunted spruce on the east side of the pass and reined his buckskin off the road. There was a level stretch here where the stage always made a brief stop. He dismounted, shivering a little, for it was cold at this altitude even in August. He rolled a smoke, considering the slowly approaching stage.

This wasn't the sort of job Kim liked. Too many people involved who had no part in the business, and he had his doubts that the man he wanted would be on the stage. Besides, Johnny Naylor, who was riding shotgun, was an unpredictable gent who might decide to be a hero. But when a man was drawing gun wages from a boss like Peg Cody, he didn't question his orders. Not if he liked his job, and Kim liked this job pretty well. There might be a future with Peg and her Clawhammer spread. She was single, pretty, and in need of a man like Kim Logan.

Kim led his horse behind a spine of rock and waited. The stage came laboring on up the steep grade and stopped.

"You can see for yourself there ain't no trouble," the driver was saying. "You're getting so jumpy you'll be shooting at shadows."

Kim stepped into view, his .44 palmed.

"A little trouble, Butch. Take it easy, Johnny."

The driver cursed. Johnny Naylor shouted— "Logan!"—in a scared voice. Jumpy, all right, and dangerous.

"I told you to take it easy, Johnny," Kim said. "You've got a wife. Butch, you've got three kids and a wife. I'd hate like blazes to make some widows and orphans today."

"All right, let's see what he wants, Johnny." The driver hunched forward on the high seat. "But I'm telling you one thing, Logan. The sheriff'll trail you to perdition, and don't figure on the Clawhammer being big enough to save your hide."

Kim had had his look at the passengers. His man was here. "You've got a fellow I want," he said. "Yuma, step down."

"Kidnapping!" Johnny Naylor cried. "You're loco, Logan. The box is plumb heavy. Why ain't you taking it?"

"I ain't a thief. You oughta know that, Johnny. And, Butch, you don't need to say anything to Ed Lane. I'm saving a man's life. Even our chuckle-headed star-toter wouldn't jail a man for that. Yuma, I ain't telling you again. Step down!"

There were three passengers—a drummer Kim had seen in Ganado, a fat woman with a cart-wheel hat who looked as if she were close to fainting, and a little man with a deeply lined face scoured by wind and sun to a dark brown. The little man would be Yuma Bill. He would be tough if pushed too far, Kim judged, and for a moment it was touch and go.

"And who would you be saving my life from?" the little man demanded.

"Some gents you never heard of," Kim answered, "but I'm saving it all right. Take my word for it."

Still Yuma Bill made no move to get out of the coach. His right hand was not in sight.

"What's this Clawhammer you're talking about?" he asked.

Kim grinned. He liked a man who had nerve, and this old Yuma Bill figured things before he made a play.

"Clawhammer's my outfit," Kim said. "A woman named Peg Cody runs it."

"Don't let that fool you!" Johnny Naylor cried. "She's as tough as Logan."

"Clawhammer," Yuma Bill murmured. "Peg Cody. Them names don't mean nothin' to me."

"Maybe the name Brit Bonham does," Kim said.

"Yeah," Yuma agreed, "it does." He swung the coach door open and stepped down, a shoe box clutched in his left hand. "Roll 'em, driver. I'll go along with this Logan."

"You're loco . . . ," Johnny Naylor began.

"Shut up!" the driver shouted, and kicked off the brake. The silk flowed out and cracked with pistol sharpness, and, as the coach lumbered on over the pass, the fat woman quietly fainted.

Yuma Bill held out his hand. "Things must be doing over here in this country. Wilder'n tarnation, Brit wrote."

"Plenty wild," Kim agreed, gripping the outstretched hand. He nodded at the shoe box. "Got your lunch there?"

The little man's faded blue eyes narrowed as doubt flowed across his face.

"Yeah, my lunch," he said.

"Well, throw it away. We'll pick up a bit of grub on the other side of the pass."

"If you don't mind," Yuma said, "I'll hang onto it."

"Sandwiches for Brit Bonham maybe," Kim murmured, and turned toward the rock ledge.

Yuma followed, and, when he saw there was only one horse, he asked: "Figgering on me walking?"

"I'll get a horse for you on the other side of the pass. We'll ride double that far. You never know how a job like this is goin' to turn out. I didn't want to leave a horse if I had to make a run for it."

The little man nodded. "Now suppose you tell me what I'm heading into."

"Nothing, I hope. I aim to deliver you to Brit Bonham at Ganado. Then you'll hear the stage was held up twice today, and you'll thank me for taking you off."

They mounted, Yuma Bill hanging tightly onto his shoe box. He remained silent until they were over the pass. Then he said: "I knowed Brit right well when he had a bank in Las Animas, and he was never one to get into trouble."

"They've got law in Las Animas," Kim said. "On Pass Creek a man packs his law on his hip. That leaves Brit in bad shape."

"Who's building a fire under him?"

"Ever heard of a gent named Hank Dunning?" Kim asked. "Or the HD outfit?"

"No."

"You will if you hang around. Takes pretty long steps, Hank does."

They rode in silence for a time, dropping fast as they angled southwest. An hour later the trail curled through a stand of aspens, and Kim pulled up at the edge of a slick rock rim that fell away a sheer hundred feet. The slope directly below was covered with pine, but farther to the west the timber played out. It was a rough country below the pines, sparsely covered by cedars and piñons and broken by ridges reaching into the valley.

"This rim goes all around the west side of the valley," Kim said, "but you'll get the best look from right here you'll get anywhere. That silver ribbon you see down there is Pass Creek. The valley is Pass Creek Valley, and right in the middle you'll see some buildings. That's Ganado, or what's left of it. Used to be a big mining camp, but it's just a cow town now."

Yuma Bill studied the long flat sweep of the valley, made a little hazy now by dust and smoke from some distant forest fire. "Where's them ranches you were talking about?" he asked.

"The Clawhammer's on this side, the HD's on the other, and both stay on their side of the creek. You can't see the buildings from here."

"A mighty big valley for two ranches," Yuma said.

"There's some little outfits scattered around, but they don't cut much ice."

"You say the Clawhammer is run by a woman?"

"That's right." Kim swung his horse back into the trail. "We'll get there, come evening."

"I thought you were taking me to Ganado."

"I didn't say when."

"Cuss it, Brit wrote like he was in a hurry for . . ."—Yuma Bill stopped, then added—"for me to get there."

"Now maybe he is, but I work for Peg Cody, so I take orders from her. She said to bring you to the Clawhammer."

"Why?"

"You'll have to ask her."

Kim felt the sharp pressure of a gun muzzle shoved against his spine.

"You're taking orders from me," Yuma Bill said flatly. "We're going to Ganado. Savvy?"

"Sure," Kim said, "but we'll take the long way. Now if that don't suit you, go ahead and blow my backbone in two. Then you'll play hob getting to Ganado. Alive, I mean." He turned his head and gave Yuma Bill a grin. "You won't be real popular around that burg. Not with Hank Dunning anyway. He'll have a reception committee waiting when he hears you weren't on the stage for his boys to pick off."

"All right." Yuma replaced his gun. "Maybe you're hoorawing me, maybe not. I'll find out."

"One thing I ain't clear on," Kim said. "Your coming to Pass Creek is about as smart as sticking your head into a bear trap. What's it goin' to buy you?"

"Not a blasted thing," the little man said, "but I'm hoping I can save Brit's hide."

"And get your carcass full of lead."

"I'll take that chance. I've owed him something for a long time, and I reckon I'm the only one he could get help from. I couldn't turn him down."

"I'll deliver that shoe box with Brit's sandwiches. You can catch the stage back to Del Norte. Or go on to Durango if you want to."

"I'll see it through to the finish," Yuma said. "In my book a man pays a debt personal."

The trail followed the rim for half a mile, then swung through a break to the pines below. Near noon they reached a small park with a log house and barn and corrals set in the center.

"What's this?" Yuma asked.

"Shorty Avis's place. One of them little outfits I was talking about. This one is here because Peg Cody lets it. Same as all the others on this side of the creek."

They rode toward the cabin.

"Rocky!" Kim called.

A girl stepped out, a Winchester held on the ready. "Who you got there?"

Kim reined up and Yuma Bill slid down.

"I just met the stage," Kim said. "Yuma, meet Shamrock Avis, and don't be fooled by her size. Don't take much dynamite to blow a man to pieces."

Yuma lifted his hat. "Pleased to meet you, ma'am."

Frowning, the girl pinned dark eyes on the little man as if making a judgment of him. "Glad to know you, mister, but if you call me Shamrock, I'll blow up in your face."

Kim laughed. "You see, Yuma? Poison, she is. Her mother named her Shamrock, but she's got other ideas, so folks call her Rocky."

"My mother, God rest her soul, made one big mistake in her life. That was naming me."

"Where's your pa?" Kim asked.

She gave him a questioning look, then said: "Out."

"Then you can feed a couple of strays. Yuma here has got a lunch, but he's saving it. Danged selfish, I claim."

"Sure, I'll rustle some grub," the girl said, "only I'll have a tough time explaining to Pa where it went to." Rocky turned into the cabin.

"What's this about her dad?" Yuma Bill asked softly.

"He just don't cotton to having anybody around who works for the Clawhammer. Plumb proddy, Shorty is, but, if I was in his boots, I wouldn't

55

want to be living on the fringe of Clawhammer range, neither." Kim motioned to the cabin. "Go on in and get acquainted. I'll put up my horse."

Kim loitered outside the log barn after he had fed and watered his horse. It was pleasantly warm now, but clouds were rolling up above the Dragon Peaks. By mid-afternoon a storm would strike with a flurry of lightning and booming of thunder and a sharp downpour. Then the sky would clear and the freshly washed earth would steam under a hot sun.

Kim had been over most of the West, but this, to his way of thinking, was the most perfect spot he had ever seen. He liked the pines, the tiny-leaved aspens that shivered with each breath of wind, the columbines and mariposa lilies that were blooming now. The wild smell of the high country seemed to satisfy some inner hunger. And he liked Rocky Avis who was as unspoiled and natural as the country. He thought of Shorty Avis who, by the grace of the Clawhammer, took a precarious living from the wilderness. A little money invested in good stock could make this a profitable spread, but Shorty had no money. If he or his neighbors did spread out, Peg Cody would start making it rough for them. There was a chance she would anyhow when she quit feuding with Hank Dunning. The Clawhammer could use the mesa for summer range.

Rocky was breaking eggs into a frying pan when

Kim came into the cabin. Yuma Bill, his shoe box on his lap, was saying: "I just can't figure this business out. Brit Bonham was never one to make trouble for anybody, and it ain't right for him to be having trouble now."

Kim stopped in the doorway, a bony shoulder pressed against the jamb, and took off his hat. He was a tall man with a lean face that was weathered to the color of dark leather. He brushed back a stubborn lock of straw-colored hair that fell across his forehead, his blue eyes pinned on the girl's straight back. Rocky Avis, he thought, fitted the life she lived. It was rough, even the furniture in the cabin was homemade. Luxuries familiar to Peg Cody in her sprawling ranch house were unknown to Rocky. But somehow Kim had the notion that Rocky would take everything just the way it was if the choice were hers to make.

Rocky, turning, saw Kim. She frowned as she set plates on the table, then straightened to face him. "When it comes to trouble," she said, "you can get all the answers from Kim. Trouble is his business."

Yuma Bill glanced at Kim's face and lowered his gaze to the black-butted .44 holstered low on his thigh.

"I figured it was," he said, "but I still can't add it all up and get a sensible answer. It's Brit who's having the trouble, ain't it?"

"Brit Bonham's having trouble, all right," the girl said evenly, "and so are a lot of other folks. Kim, he can smell trouble as far as a hound dog can smell 'coon."

"It's Brit Bonham I want to know about," the little man said. "What's that got to do with Logan?"

"Everything. A year ago Kim rode into the Clawhammer and told Peg Cody he'd heard she needed a snake stomper. For a hundred dollars a month he'd stomp her snakes for her, and she's been paying him that ever since."

Kim hung his hat on a peg and dropped into a rawhide-bottom chair. "When you get done gabbing about me, you'd better take a look at them eggs, Shamrock. I sure do hate burned eggs."

"You call me Shamrock again," the girl cried furiously, "and you'll get your eggs down the back of your neck!"

Kim laughed softly. "I told you how it was, Yuma. There ain't even a mountain lion in these parts that'll look her in the eye."

Rocky, facing the stove, said in the same angry voice: "Look at him, wearing fancy Justins and a Stetson that set him back fifty dollars. Silver spurs. He's even got gold in his teeth. Nobody else can afford stuff like that but Kim Logan."

"What are you getting so heated up for?" Kim asked. "I ain't robbed a bank."

58

"You're working for Peg Cody. Same thing." Rocky spooned the eggs into a platter that held a dozen pieces of salt side. She slammed the platter down on the table. "You wouldn't know how it is, trying to make a living when any minute Peg Cody may take it into her head to run all of us off and take over our places."

"You're just dreaming," Kim said mildly. "Peg's never bothered you."

"I'm not dreaming, I'm nightmaring." She pulled a pan of biscuits out of the oven, placed the biscuits on a plate, and set them on the table. "It isn't just Peg that makes me so mad. I know what to expect from a greedy woman. It's you I can't figure out. You've been doing what you call snake stomping all your life. What's it got you besides fancy duds?"

"I get along," Kim said, still mild.

"Sure. You could drift out of here tomorrow and put everything you own in your pockets. You haven't got a dollar in the bank. You don't own a cow. Not even a calf. You could come here and work for thirty a month and beans, but that would mean chasing cows through the scrub oak, and you're no brush popper. You . . . you're just a snake stomper."

She picked up the coffee pot and filled their cups, and flounced back to the stove again.

"Come on and eat." She dropped into a chair, shoulders sagging as if suddenly tired. "I guess

59

that anywhere we went, there'd be greedy people like Peg Cody and Hank Dunning. It's just that you seem different, Kim."

"Reckon I never thought about it," Kim said.

II

There was no more talk for a time. Kim and Yuma Bill ate, Kim wondering what had got into the girl. He had never seen her so angry, and apparently over nothing at all. When he was finished, he rolled a smoke, eyes on Rocky's white face.

"What set you off?" he asked.

"Nothing much." She filled their coffee cups. "I just got to thinking about Brit Bonham who used his bank to help folks. Little folks like us along with the big ones like Peg Cody. Now look at what he got himself into."

"I'm tired of being in the dark," Yuma Bill said. "What kind of trouble is Brit in?"

"Dunning aims to . . . ," Rocky began.

"I'll tell it," Kim cut in. "He loaned too much money. That's all. Peg borrowed thirty thousand to stock her range. The Clawhammer was in debt and pretty well run down when her old man died. So when she borrowed from Brit, she went whole hog. Too much, cattle prices being what they are. Looks like she and Brit are going broke together."

"She could save a hundred dollars a month by firing you," Rocky said sharply.

Kim shook his head. "I ain't flattering myself too much, I reckon, when I say she needs me. Dunning would start pushing tomorrow if I wasn't around."

"What do you think he's doing now?" the girl cried.

Kim grinned at her. "He's just warming up to the job."

"You mean you've got Dunning bluffed?" Yuma Bill asked.

"Sort of. You see, he's a scheming son-of-a-bitch. Fighting a woman is his size. Long as I'm workin' for the Clawhammer, he ain't got a sure thing."

"He has if Peg doesn't fire Dutch Heinz," Rocky said. "I'd bet my bottom dollar he's sold out to Dunning."

Kim rose. "Let's ride, Yuma."

"You'd sure better." Shorty Avis was standing in the doorway, a cocked Winchester in his hands. "I told you before you wasn't wanted here. Now git, 'fore I put a round window in your skull."

"Take it easy," Kim said. "You've got no quarrel with me."

"I've got a quarrel with the Clawhammer!" Avis bellowed. "Git, I said."

He was a tough bantam, this Shorty Avis, with a knobby face and piercing black eyes that were alive with fury. Although Avis had never been friendly, Kim liked him because he instinctively liked any man who had courage. Shorty Avis had it, or he wouldn't be here telling Clawhammer men to stay off his land.

"Tell him, Dad," Rocky said quietly. "I was going to, but I hadn't got around to it."

Kim swung to face the girl. "Tell me what?"

"I'll tell you all right," Shorty barked. "You betcha I will. Dutch Heinz was up here early this morning. Said we had to get out of the country. Offered me a hundred dollars for this quarter section. Well, I ain't stirring my stumps, Logan! You go tell that woman you work for."

Kim studied Avis a moment, finding this hard to believe. Peg had never indicated she would oust the little fry.

"I'll talk to Peg," Kim said finally. "It don't smell right."

"Nothing smells right about the Clawhammer." Avis gave him a wicked grin. "But I ain't goin' to worry about you. Dunning will get you 'fore sundown. I'm betting on it."

Kim sensed triumph in the man. "Keep talking, Shorty," he said.

"I'll enjoy talking, and I'll enjoy seeing the finish. I sure won't lose no tears when they plant you."

Kim put on his hat. "You know something, Shorty?"

"You bet I know something." Avis backed out of the doorway. "Won't be long till you find out all about it. Now dust."

"What do you know, Dad?" Rocky asked, and, when her father's lips tightened into a stubborn line, she said with some sharpness: "Kim is taking a friend of Brit Bonham's into Ganado. In case you've forgotten, Brit is the best friend we have on this range."

"Now wait a minute," Kim said. "Have I done anything to make you think I wasn't your friend?"

"You're taking Peg Cody's orders," Rocky said.

He looked down at the girl's defiant face. "That don't mean I ain't a friend of yours."

"You won't be anybody's friend for long," Shorty said. "Dunning sent Phil Martin over here with five HD hands. They're hunting for you now."

It took Kim a moment to grasp the significance fully. There had been a good deal of sparring between the Clawhammer and the HD in the year Kim had been in the valley, but not once had a Clawhammer man crossed the creek on HD range, nor had HD riders crossed to the Clawhammer side. Now, if Martin, Dunning's ramrod, had come hunting for Kim, it must mean that Dunning had decided it was time to wind things up.

"Where are they?" Kim asked.

"Indian Springs the last I saw of 'em."

Kim stepped out of the cabin. "Let me have a horse, Shorty. We can't dodge 'em riding double."

"Thought you had a horse for me," Yuma said angrily.

"I have. At the Clawhammer."

"You mean you figured on me riding double all the way to your cursed ranch?" Yuma Bill shouted.

Kim swung to face him. "I didn't figure you'd be on that stage. Didn't make sense that a stranger would come toting a bunch of *dinero* into this country just to help out an old coot like Brit Bonham."

"Let him take Blackie, Pa," Rocky said.

Shorty Avis began to swell up. "When I let a Clawhammer man take a horse of mine, I'll be fit for the asylum!"

"You're fit for it if you don't," Rocky cut in. "It's Brit Bonham's friend who needs the horse. Anyhow, if we stay here, it will be because Kim helps us."

"Help us!" Avis howled. "Why, this gun-totin' varmint wouldn't help his own grandmother if that Cody woman told him to steal the gold teeth out of her head."

Kim started toward the barn, calling over his shoulder: "Fetch your sandwiches and come on, Yuma."

"You touch my horse and I'll . . . !" Avis bawled.

"You'll do nothing!" Rocky cried.

Yuma Bill caught up with Kim. "I hope that girl runs the roost," he said.

"She does," Kim said.

He threw gear on Shorty Avis's black gelding, tightened the cinches on the buckskin, and swung up.

"Let's ride."

Yuma Bill mounted, the shoe box gripped under one arm. They left the clearing on the run, Kim lifting a hand to Rocky. He had one glance at Shorty's knobby face, filled with a dark and forbidding anger. He grinned, knowing the man would do nothing more than rail at his daughter, for, when the chips were down, it was Rocky who called the turn. Then Kim and Yuma Bill were in the aspens, the trail dropping swiftly toward the valley below.

Kim kept a fast pace. An hour after leaving the Avis place, he and Yuma Bill reached a stand of pines, and here the trail ran directly down the slope. It was an old Ute trail that the Avises and their closest neighbors, the Fawcetts, used on their trips to town. Kim pulled up, motioning for Yuma Bill to do the same. As he sat listening, the little man's eyes were pinned on him.

Indian Springs lay to the right. Probably Phil Martin had stopped Shorty Avis there. If Avis had known where Kim was, he would have told the HD man, for Avis wasn't smart enough to see that, if Hank Dunning smashed the Clawhammer, he would take the entire valley. Then Avis and the rest of the small fry would be worse off than they were now. Peg Cody was greedy, as Rocky Avis had said, but she lacked Dunning's driving ruthlessness.

"How far to the Clawhammer?" Yuma Bill asked.

" 'Bout three hours from here," Kim said, "if we went straight, but I don't figure we can. Chances are Martin and his bunch is off there somewhere." He motioned toward the southwest. "I'll feel a lot better when I know exactly where they are."

"You reckon they're after me?"

Kim shook his head. "Me. Dunning will figure his boys got you, but I've been worrying him ever since I got here. If they can make wolf meat out of me here in the hills, it'll be safer and maybe easier than doing the job in town."

"How would they know where to look?"

"I ride through these hills all the time. Part of my job is seeing that HD men stay on their side of the creek."

"Suppose they get you?"

Kim shrugged. "Then they'll move in. Our hands are with the cattle in the high country. Just Peg and an old man at the ranch. Chances are Dunning will burn the buildings, figuring Peg will sell for any offer he makes."

"Why, she wouldn't quit that easy, would she?"

"I ain't sure," Kim said thoughtfully. "She talks pretty tough, but she's never been through a range war. Her old man used to be the big push in the valley, but now the shoe's on the other foot."

"Hasn't she got a crew and a ramrod?"

"She's got a crew, but they ain't a salty outfit. And Dutch Heinz, the ramrod, claims he ain't a fighting man."

There was no point in telling Yuma Bill he had never been sure of Dutch Heinz and was less sure now. He still found it hard to believe that Peg had sent Heinz to warn Shorty Avis out of the country. It might be Dunning's idea to force the small ranchers into a war against the Clawhammer. It would be like Dunning to get someone else to do his fighting for him.

"I don't savvy," Yuma Bill said. "Looks like this valley's big enough for both of 'em."

"Not for them it ain't," Kim said.

He took a parallel course to the trail for a time. Phil Martin was a methodical sort who would systematically comb the hills, spreading his hands out to cover the most ground. If Shorty Avis had not warned him, Kim would have ridden squarely into the HD guns. But now there was a chance he could slip through them.

The ground leveled off and Kim reined up again. He hipped around in the saddle.

"Smell anything?"

Yuma nodded. "Dust. They've been through here."

"And they ain't far away." Kim motioned. "Ganado Creek is on the other side of this ridge.

The cañon's deep. We don't want to get run into it. Come on."

They circled a barrier of rocks and came again into the thick timber. Ten minutes later they broke out of the pines into a small park. An HD man was riding directly toward them, a burly cowhand named Tonto Miles.

For an instant all three were too stunned by surprise to do anything. Then Miles let out a squall, pulled his gun, and fired, the bullet going high and wide. He cracked steel to his horse as Kim threw a slug at him and missed. Then he disappeared into the timber toward the trail.

"They're all around us," Kim said in disgust. "Ran smack into 'em."

Other shouts sounded, and there was the thunder of hoofs as Kim put his horse into a run and headed directly across the clearing. Just before he reached the timber, he looked back. Yuma Bill was ten feet behind him. Four men had reached the far side of the park, Phil Martin in the lead.

Whatever thought Kim had of making a fight of it left him. He had no idea how Yuma Bill would pan out in a showdown. Even if he was good, the odds were still too long.

Kim slanted downgrade, hoping to get out of the rough country. If they could reach the flat, there was a chance they could outrun Martin's bunch, but the valley was still a long way off. Besides, there was no telling how many others there were, or where they were. Shorty Avis had said six, but he might not have seen all of them, and Hank Dunning was not a man to do a half job.

Almost immediately Kim was forced to reverse direction, for two riders came into view directly in front of him. He angled back toward the rim.

"Come on!" he called to Yuma Bill.

He knew now there was no way to avoid a fight, but it would be on a battleground he picked. Here the pines were small and scattering. Martin and the three riders with him remained in sight, the distance between them unchanged. The other two had altered their course to parallel Kim's and Yuma Bill's, apparently aiming to block their escape to open country.

A mesa hill loomed ahead.

"You're letting 'em run us into a bottleneck!" Yuma Bill bawled.

A gun cracked behind them, but the distance was too great and the bullet fell short. They reached the mesa hill and slanted up it, their horses laboring, red dust kicked up into a cloud. Another gun roared. This bullet came too close for comfort. The climb had slowed Kim and Yuma Bill, and Martin had cut the distance between them.

They topped the crest and Kim waved for Yuma Bill to go on. He reined up, drawing his gun. Martin, ahead of the others, had reached the base of the hill. He looked up, close enough for Kim to see his broad face clearly, the sweeping sand-colored mustache, the crooked nose, even the smudge of red dust across his right cheek.

Martin gave a frantic yell when he saw Kim's gun sweep down. He jerked his horse to a stop and plunged out of saddle just as Kim fired. He dived toward a boulder as Kim squeezed off a second shot. Then he was under cover, flat against the ground, and Kim was not sure whether he had scored a hit either time.

The three men following Martin were firing, but it was too far for accurate shooting with handguns. Kim wheeled toward his horse and snaked his Winchester from the boot, thinking that this might be as good a place as any to make a stand. He could keep Martin nailed behind the boulder until dark.

For the moment Kim had forgotten the other two riders who had bobbed up in front of them. Yuma Bill had swung back, yelling: "Come on, you idiot! They'll pot us like two ducks in a puddle."

Then Kim remembered. He looked for the two men, but they had disappeared. A slab of rock ran like an unbroken red wall from the base of the hill to the crest. They must have reined in behind it and were climbing to the top. Probably they wouldn't go that far. They would dismount and hole up behind the rock slab. Then it would be as Yuma Bill said. The HD men would be forted up while Kim and Yuma Bill were in the open.

Kim whirled back to his horse and shoved the Winchester into the boot.

"I told you to hightail!" he shouted.

"I never went off and left a man in a tight in my life!" Yuma Bill shot back. "What in blazes do you think I am?"

Kim swung into leather, motioning toward the rim that enclosed the east side of the valley.

"Dust!" he called. "We'll make 'em come after us."

The cliff rose sheer above the mesa, a nest of boulders at its base. Kim pointed his horse toward the rocks. Yuma Bill swung in beside him, his angry voice rising above the *clatter* of hoofs. "You aiming to fly to the top?"

"Save your wind! We'll fort up."

III

Hoofs beating against the rocky ground, Kim and Yuma rode hard. When they were out of gun range, Kim pulled his buckskin down and looked back. No one was in sight. They reached the boulders and swung in behind them. There was protection of a sort here, for the cliff formed an overhang so that the horses could be safely left at the base without danger of being seen from the rim.

Stepping down, Kim pulled his Winchester from

the boot. "Take the horses back there." He motioned to the cliff. "Keep 'em there."

"Wait a minute, you danged chuckle-headed . . . ," Yuma Bill began.

But Kim didn't wait. He climbed to the top of the largest boulder and dropped flat on its smooth, weather-worn surface, eyes scanning the rocky flat in front of him. Still no one was in sight.

The ridge was about a mile long, with a steep drop-off on every side except the east end that butted against the cliff. It was covered by sagebrush, broken only occasionally by a wind-gnarled cedar. Westward beyond the break-off another steep slope dropped to the level floor of the valley. Kim could see the valley, bright, green where the sunlight was upon it, or freckled by islands of shadow. Clouds were boiling up now in a dark forbidding mass from the sullen Dragon Peaks. In an hour the clouds would cover the sky, and the sunlight would be blotted out. Ganado Cañon lay just to the south, an ugly gash that ran from the great peaks of the Continental Divide to the valley. There its walls disappeared, and the creek that tumbled with white-laced violence from the altitude slowed its course to meander across the valley.

Already the storm was moving in. Lightning had begun to flash in weird shifting veins above the Dragons, and thunder was rolling out its deep booming, muted somewhat by distance. In one way this sage-carpeted flat was a good position. Martin would find a direct attack difficult and costly, for the flat offered no adequate shelter for man or horse. On the other hand, this boulder where Kim lay might be a place of death. There was a break in the cliff to Kim's right. If an HD man climbed to the rim, he could look directly down on the boulder. But right or wrong, Kim had picked his spot, and here the battle would be fought out to a decision.

The minutes dragged while the sky darkened and the ominous roll of thunder came closer. Then Kim heard the grating sound of boots on the side of the boulder. Yuma Bill was climbing toward him.

"I told you to stay with the horses!"

Yuma Bill dropped down beside Kim. "They'll stay where I left 'em. Now maybe you'd like to tell me why you holed up here."

"Where would you be wanting to go?" Kim flung a hand toward the flat. "Out there maybe?"

"We could have kept riding. If they had poked their heads up over the hill, we'd have blowed 'em off their necks."

"About the time we got far enough out there for them two *hombres* to notch their sights on us, we'd have got our own heads blowed off. This was the only place we could keep out of their sight unless you wanted to go on down into Ganado Cañon, which I didn't."

Yuma Bill scowled, gaze swinging toward the lip of the cañon. "Reckon I forgot about that hole in the ground."

Kim jabbed a finger in the direction of the valley. "The Clawhammer's off there. Just below where the creek comes out of the cañon. I figured we'd hole up here till dark, then make a run for it."

"How about the rim?" Yuma Bill jerked a \thumb at the sullen red cliff behind them.

"That's the joker," Kim admitted. "If Martin's got a mountain goat in his outfit, he'll climb up there and we'll be caught like your two ducks in a puddle."

Yuma Bill rolled a smoke and fired it.

"Logan," he said, "all that means anything to you is the hundred dollars a month you're getting, but I'm in this tight because I want to help a friend who gave me a hand once. I'm going to Ganado, and I don't aim to sit here till dark."

"You sure won't do Bonham no good if Martin plugs you and nabs your lunch box," Kim said.

"Brit's letter sounded like he didn't have much time," Yuma said sourly, "and here we are, nailed down on top of a blasted rock."

"You want to stay alive, don't you?" Kim demanded.

Yuma Bill glanced at the cliff behind him. "I ain't sure I will."

"Get back with the horses," Kim said irritably.

"Maybe you need some help to stay alive. And

I'd never get to that town if I struck out alone."

Kim's eyes had been searching the flat. He sat up, Winchester across his lap. "Take a look, friend. Five of 'em. Martin's back with them."

The HD riders had come into view where the rock slab leveled out on the flat. They reined up, motionless, as they studied the cliffs. Kim could not tell whether he and Yuma Bill had been seen or not, but it seemed unlikely that Martin would close in.

"Five," Yuma Bill muttered. "Where is the other one?"

"Chances are he's crawling to the top," Kim answered. "It'll take him an hour or so. By that time we'll be under the overhang."

"Then we can't watch the other five and they'll walk in on us," Yuma said dourly. "I don't like it, Logan."

"I ain't in love with this deal, either. What do you want to do . . . make a run for it?"

Yuma shook his head. "Not with them kind of odds."

They sat watching Martin and his men who had come on and stopped just short of rifle range. Kim considered taking a few shots to worry them, and decided against it. The only shells that he had for the Winchester were those in the magazine, and he'd need those and more before dark.

He gave some thought to climbing to the rim so Yuma Bill's back would be protected, and gave it up. The only break in the cliff for a mile or more to either side was a long trough-like slot that furnished precarious footing. If the other HD man had already started up, a climber below him would make a clear target.

There was nothing to do but wait, and Kim never found waiting easy. Nor did Yuma Bill like it. He kept shifting, smoking incessantly, eyes on the HD men who had dismounted and were hunkered in a tight little knot in front of their horses.

"Damn it!" Yuma burst out. "I'm goin' to ride out there and talk to 'em. You said it was you they wanted."

"Go ahead," Kim said. "You'll get halfway there if you're lucky and their shooting ain't good."

The little man beat a hand against the rock. "You haven't told me all of this."

"No," Kim admitted, "but I'll tell you now. Brit Bonham's spread himself so far that folks got to talking. It's my guess Dunning got the talk going, aiming to start a rush on the bank. Bonham ain't got the cash to pay off his depositors, so he'll have to close. He'll call in his loans. That breaks Peg Cody."

"So that's why you were so interested in keeping me alive?"

Kim nodded. "Only I don't figure it'll go quite like that. Dunning is a big depositor. If he pulls his money out, Bonham's finished. So Dunning will make Bonham an offer for Peg's notes, and Bonham will have to sell 'em."

Yuma Bill tapped fingertips against the rock. "If I get my cash to Brit in time, I'll save the bank, and, while I'm doing that, I save the Clawhammer."

"That's the size of it," Kim said. "Bonham told Peg when he was expecting you. Like a fool, he told Dunning, too. That's why we figured you'd never get to Ganado alive if I didn't stop the stage, on the off chance you'd be on it."

"I still don't savvy why you're taking me all over, to get me to town," Yuma said sulkily.

"Reckon Peg wants to thank you." Kim grinned. "She's got a right nice way of thanking men who are on her side, but she's hard on the others."

It began to rain, a driving downpour with lightning breaking across the sky in vivid leaping flashes.

"Come on!" Kim shouted above the rolling thunder. "We've got to keep that lunch box dry, or your sandwiches will sure get damp."

Kim slid off the rock and dived under the overhang, Yuma Bill following. It was dry there, for there was little wind, and the rain was coming straight down.

"Won't last long." Kim leaned his Winchester against the sandstone cliff, and untied his slicker from behind the saddle. "Stay here. This might be what they've been waiting for."

He stepped back into the rain, circling the big

boulder instead of climbing to the top. He hunkered in front of it, his back hard against its wet surface so that a man on the rim above would have to lean out to see him.

The rain had spread a silver curtain across the flat, pelting it with fierce violence and hiding the five HD men out there. The summer storms seldom lasted more than a few minutes, but it might be long enough to give the Martin rider the cover he needed.

A Winchester *cracked* from the rim, the bullet striking the rock and screaming off into space. Kim pressed back against the boulder. The beat of hoofs sweeping in from the sage flat came clearly to him between the rolls of thunder. They had timed it perfectly. He was caught between the men riding in and the one on the rim.

He glimpsed them, shrouded by rain. He must have eased forward as he brought the Winchester to his shoulder, for the man on the rim squeezed off another shot, the slug slicing across the boulder, sending rock splinters flying. Kim began firing.

It was poor shooting, for the light was thin and the HD men were low in their saddles and riding fast. Kim missed with his first bullet, tagged Martin with his second, and missed with a third.

A slug from the rim slapped into the ground in front of him. A quick gust of wind swept the rain against him, blinding him for a moment. He squeezed his eyes shut and opened them, shaking his head and swearing.

Martin's men were angling a little now as they opened up with their Colts, bullets peppering the rock around Kim. He pronged back the hammer \of his Winchester and squeezed off another shot knocking an HD rider out of his saddle.

A scream of wild terror sounded shrilly through the heavy roar of guns. A body *thudded* into the rocks to Kim's left, but he had no time to see who it was. He was working his Winchester steadily. He heard Yuma Bill cut loose with his Colt. A moment later the fight had been won. Martin had stopped to help the fallen man up behind him, right arm swinging in a wide signal for retreat.

"That yahoo on the rim fell off," Yuma Bill, beside Kim, was saying. "Sure got busted up."

Another Winchester was *cracking* from the rim, but the bullets were not slanting down at Kim and Yuma Bill. They were being aimed at the HD riders who were in full retreat across the flat. Kim emptied his rifle at them. He did not know how much damage he had inflicted on Martin's crew, but it must have been considerable to have knocked the fight out of them so effectively.

Kim rose, glancing at Yuma Bill who was staring after the retreating HD crew. The little man wiped the rain from his face, blinking. "Who's up there?" he asked.

"I don't know, but I've got a hunch."

Kim glanced at the broken body of the man who had fallen. He had seen the fellow in Ganado with Phil Martin, but didn't know his name. Just a gun-handy drifter who had taken Dunning's wages and made a bad bargain. As Kim ran past him to his horse, a thought cut its way through his mind: *It could be me lying there.*

He slipped his Winchester into the boot and, stepping into saddle, brought his buckskin around. He rode out of the shelter of the overhang into the rain. It had slacked off now to a fine mist and the lightning was gone from the sky. The storm had moved on, but the smell of rain was heavy in the air and the red sandstone cliff was wet and bright.

"What are you up to?" Yuma Bill shouted.

"Finding something out," Kim said.

He rode directly away from the cliff until he could see the rim. Rocky Avis was standing there, a slim boyish figure in a man's shirt and trousers, a rifle in her hand. She waved when she saw Kim.

"Both of you all right?" she called.

"Nary a scratch," he answered, reining his horse around. "How'd you come to buy into this ruckus?"

"I figured it was a good idea to keep you two alive," she said. "I got up on the rim after you left and watched them give you a run. Then, when you forted up down there, I thought you might need a hand, so I rode over. What about that hairpin who went over the edge?"

"Dead."

She shook her head. "I'm sorry."

"What for? He wouldn't have been sorry if he'd plugged me or Yuma in the back."

"I know, but it seems a poor thing to die for. He was leaning over, trying to get a bead on you when I saw him. I got up close before he knew I was there. I told him to hook the moon. He jumped and took a step back and over he went."

"Well, you sure did a job for us. It would have been a little rough if they'd kept coming in." He cuffed back his hat. "Rocky, this ain't good. You're into the fight now if they saw who you were."

"We're in the fight anyway. Pa's just too stubborn to see it. You two better get along now."

"We'll have to take the body in."

"Tie him on his horse. I'll have Pa take him to town. You'd better make tracks while you can. They might still give you trouble."

Kim shook his head. "They had aplenty, but we'll find his horse and leave him here. You hightail home, and get it through Shorty's head that Dunning's the man he'd better be scared of."

"I'll tell him, but he won't believe it. Not after seeing Dutch Heinz this morning."

She waved and disappeared over the rim. Kim rode back to Yuma Bill.

"It was Rocky Avis," he said. "She don't see this business like Shorty does. She trailed us, figuring we might need a hand."

"So a woman saves our lives," the little man said. "I don't like that, Logan."

"I do. It was kind of touchy there for a minute."

"Most women don't forget what you owe 'em," Yuma said bitterly. "I know."

"Rocky's different," Kim said, and rode past Yuma Bill to the break in the cliff.

The dead man's horse had been tied to a small cedar. Kim led him back to the rocks and they lashed the body across the saddle. Later, riding across the flat, steaming under a hot sun, he glanced at Yuma Bill, wondering what was in the man's mind.

Suddenly Yuma felt Kim's eyes and turned his head.

"I hope you know what you're doing!" he burst out. "If we're too late to save Brit's bank, I'll take it out of your hide."

"I'm in this to earn my hundred dollars a month, you know," Kim said. "Remember?"

"That's got nothing to do with . . ."

"I just got to thinking about what you said, then I got to asking myself how you got so high and mighty that you could preach to me."

Yuma Bill's craggy face softened. "So that's it. Well, I didn't aim to preach. Just seemed like you had things twisted a mite."

"Like what?"

"Like putting your orders above saving Brit Bonham's bank."

"I'm just doing my job. Strikes me that when a man takes a job, he'd better do it."

"That ain't enough," said Yuma. "I'm more'n twice your age, Logan. That's given me twice as much time to think as you've had. Now I ain't saying I ain't done my share of ornery things, but somewhere along the line I've found out what pays a man and what don't."

"My job pays me," Kim said, "and pretty good."

"No, you're getting short-changed unless you're in love with this Peg Cody. It's like this, Logan. Every man sows some seed, it grows, and it's goin' to be harvested whether he does it himself or someone else does. Now what kind of seed have you sowed?"

"*Aw,* get a pulpit," Kim said resentfully.

Yuma Bill smiled, and shook his head. "Well, maybe I oughta, but you started this sermon, and I aim to finish it. It's short and sweet. You get to the last hill. We all do, sooner or later, and I'm a lot closer to it than you are. You take a look back and you see all them crops you've planted. If you've used the right seed, you go over the range feeling pretty good about everything. But this other *hombre*, the one who didn't give a whoop what he planted, why, I reckon he's goin' to burn in the blazin' fire the parsons talk about."

"I suppose you know all about women, too," Kim said. "You seem to know everything else."

"I know a little, all right," Yuma said, bitterness again creeping into his voice. "I've always had a little money, and that draws women like honey draws bees." He scratched his nose. "But maybe I had your little Rocky girl all wrong. If she loves you, she won't be holding you in her debt. Some women ain't capable of love. Maybe she is."

"Love me? Why, shucks, she's just a kid!"

"Nineteen or twenty, ain't she?" Yuma shrugged. "Old enough to be in love. I can't see no other reason for her getting so huffy with you at noon if she wasn't. Or risking her hide to save yours."

It was something Kim had not thought about before, and he dismissed it as an old man's idle talk. But there was one thing he did know. The last person in the world he wanted to hurt was Rocky Avis.

IV

As the sun tipped down behind the Dragon Peaks and dusk flowed across the valley, the purple twilight gave a sense of weird unreality. Darkness moved in, and the Dragons became sharp black points against a pale sky. Then the last trace of light died, and the mountains faded into indistinct blurs.

When Kim and Yuma Bill rode down to the valley floor, the distant lights of Ganado gleamed like clustered stars dropped from the black sky. They turned toward the Clawhammer, and the lamp-brightened windows of the big ranch house came into sight. They finally reined up under the ancient cottonwoods that had prompted Peg's father to build his house here.

"Who is it?" a man called from the corrals.

A barking dog bounded toward Kim. "All right, Nero," Kim said, and, when the dog was silent, he called: "It's me, Limpy!"

The man drifted up out of the darkness.

"Any trouble, son?" he asked.

"A little," Kim said. "Peg in the house?"

"Yeah. Just got back from town. Go on in. I'll take care of your horses."

"Come on, Yuma." Kim crossed the yard and stepped up on the porch. "Scrape the mud off, Yuma. She's tough on a man who totes mud into her house."

"I respect a clean woman," Yuma Bill said, "if she don't make a religion out of it."

"She don't." Kim cleaned his boots on the scraper and went in. He called: "Peg!"

The smell of coffee and frying ham was a fragrance in the house that sharpened Kim's hunger. He crossed the living room to the kitchen door, with Yuma Bill following, the shoe box under his arm.

Peg Cody turned from the big wood range where she was frying ham, and gave Kim a quick smile. She was tall, almost as tall as Kim and about the same age. Her hair seemed even redder than usual in the lamplight, and her hazel eyes that could reflect a smile or be bright with wild and sudden anger were warm with pleasure at seeing Kim. She was a temperamental woman with a disposition that swung easily from one extreme to the other, and Kim had learned long ago to walk easily until he read her mood at the moment.

"Come in, Kim," she said. "I had a hunch you'd be dragging in as hungry as an old bear in the spring, so I fixed a little extra."

"This is Yuma Bill," Kim said. "Yuma, meet Miss Cody."

"I'm glad to know you," Peg said pleasantly. "I've been worried about both of you all day."

"Howdy, ma'am," the little man said, his voice cool.

She turned back to the stove. "Brit Bonham calls you his friend. That's the finest thing one man can call another."

Yuma Bill nodded, her words thawing him. "Thank you, ma'am. I'm proud to be Brit's friend."

She motioned toward the back door. "Wash up, Kim. Supper's ready."

On the back porch, Kim pumped a pan of water, and stepped aside for Yuma Bill to wash. He looked out across the valley that seemed to stretch into black eternity, and thought of the first time he had seen Peg a year ago. He had ridden in from Ganado on his buckskin, tired and gaunt and looking tough enough to impress the devil himself. He must have impressed Peg, for she had hired him with no more recommendation than the toughness of his appearance.

Since then he had kept on riding, but with a definite purpose. As soon as he had caught the full picture, he had told Peg there would never be peace in the valley until Hank Dunning was dead. On at least two occasions he had prodded Dunning until he thought the man would go for his gun, but the HD owner had wanted none of it. Kim had puzzled over that. Dunning did not appear to be a coward. Almost everyone in the valley was afraid of him, for he was fast with his bone-handled .45. Still, he had turned his back and walked off.

Yuma Bill emptied his pan over the railing.

"Yours, Logan," he said. He drifted back into the kitchen.

Kim washed and combed his hair, thinking that in the year he had worked for the Clawhammer he still did not really understand Peg. He had never felt the sting of her tongue, although he had seen her in towering rages when some of her riders made a mistake or failed to carry out an order. She must have sensed that he was one man who would take nothing from her.

Kim did know one thing. The Clawhammer meant everything to her. For that reason she had gambled recklessly in borrowing so much money from Bonham. But perhaps she had not considered it a gamble. She seldom discussed ranch business with Kim, and she never asked his advice. Their relationship had been strictly that of employer and employee. Still, she had the power to stir him as she could stir any normal man, and she had often gone out of her way to be with him. Yet Kim had a feeling that her deepest thoughts and ambitions were her own secrets.

"Break your leg out there?" Peg called.

He went into the kitchen, patting the stubborn cowlick that never stayed in place.

"Yeah, broke my leg," he said.

"Have to shoot you. No room on this spread for a useless horse." She motioned to a chair. "Sit down. I'm so hungry I'm going to start eating whether you two do or not."

It was a good meal of ham, beans, fried potatoes, biscuits, apple butter, and hot black coffee. Kim had never had a bad meal at her table. It was one of the many things he liked about her. She could ride a horse with the best; she made a hand when she was needed, but she also kept the house immaculate, made her own dresses, and baked the best chocolate cake he had ever tasted.

"Better fetch your crew in," Kim said, reaching for the ham. "Dunning's fixing to force a fight."

"Then he'll get one."

"I don't like the notion of you being here with just Limpy, and I won't be earning my wages if I sit here keeping the seat of my pants warm."

She frowned, throwing him a sharp glance as if not liking his advice. "I'm not afraid of Dunning, but I am worried about our cows. That's where my boys belong, and that's where they'll stay."

"We had some trouble," Kim said.

"Let's hear about it."

Kim told her what had happened, leaving out only the fact that Rocky Avis had bought into the fight. He wished he had told Yuma Bill to hold his tongue about it. Glancing now at the little man, he was relieved to see that Yuma Bill was busying himself with a cigarette, apparently satisfied to let Kim do the talking.

Peg put down her coffee cup. "I don't like it, Kim, but I've contracted to deliver five hundred head of steers in Durango this fall. I've got to do that. Nothing else is important."

"Your life is," Kim said doggedly.

"My life isn't in danger. We have law here, Kim."

"Law?" Kim laughed shortly. "What kind of law does Ed Lane give this valley? He's picked his side, and it ain't ours."

She gave him a questioning glance. "That's the way it's got to be, Kim. You're all the army I can afford to hire."

Kim rose, suddenly angry. He was a good man, but no man, regardless of how good he was, could fight Hank Dunning's outfit. It was up to every Clawhammer hand from the ramrod on down to old Limpy.

"I ain't one to tell my boss how to run her business," Kim said sharply, "but I've been through some range wars, and likewise I know about sheriffs like our great Ed Lane. When Dunning's ready to finish us off, Lane will go fishing."

"All right, Kim," she said, her tone matching his. "I hired you to use your gun. Use it."

"I will, blast it!" Kim pounded the table with his fist. "But I don't cotton to being chased by Martin and five of his boys. Call your hands down and let me take 'em across the creek. I'll finish this in one night, and then you can raise your beef in peace."

Peg was on her feet then, face red with anger. "My boys are cowhands! You're the snake stomper. Now you can either stomp or drift. This is the first time you've smelled powder smoke, and it looks like you don't care much for the smell."

Kim stalked toward the door.

"You're losing a good man, Miss Cody," Yuma Bill said quietly.

"Wait, Kim!" Peg cried, and ran after him. "I'm sorry. I shouldn't have said that."

Kim turned, glaring at her. "You're blamed right

you shouldn't have said it. Maybe you don't know it, but you're in a fight! The only way to win is to get the jump on Dunning and finish him."

"Let me think about it." She put a hand on his arm, a quick impulsive gesture. "It's just that I don't want to force trouble if I can help it. I . . . I guess the money I owe Bonham is making me crazy."

"What about Bonham?" Yuma Bill asked. "His bank all right?"

"There's been no run yet, but you'd better be in town by nine tomorrow."

"I aim to." Yuma Bill got to his feet and reached for the shoe box. "I couldn't figure out why Logan wanted to fetch me here first. I still can't, but, if Brit's all right, it don't make no difference."

"He's tired, Kim," Peg said. "Take him out to the bunkhouse. Then you come back."

She was suddenly contrite, and that was not like her. She seldom apologized about anything or admitted making a mistake, but in her way she was doing both now. A small inviting smile lay in the corners of her mouth; her eyes were half closed as if she were enjoying the anticipation of something that lay ahead.

Kim nodded and turned toward the living room door. He stopped, suddenly tense, his hand dropping to gun butt. Someone had ridden up and was crossing the yard, spurs *jingling*. Kim backed away to the table, and waited there until the man came into the kitchen. It was Dutch Heinz.

Kim glanced briefly at Yuma Bill who had set the shoe box down on the table again. Heinz stood in the doorway, spread-legged. He nodded at Peg, gave Kim a cool stare, and brought his gray eyes to Yuma Bill. He was a stocky man with a wide, flat nose, and possessed of an overbearing insolence that never failed to arouse resentment in Kim when he was around the man.

"Who's this?" Heinz asked, motioning to Yuma Bill.

"It's Bonham's friend that we were expecting," Peg said.

"Bonham's friend, eh? So Logan got him off the stage. Any trouble?"

"A little," Kim said.

Heinz walked toward the table. Yuma Bill threw a questioning glance at Kim and brought his eyes back to Heinz, his furrowed face dark with trouble.

"Things don't look good in town, Dutch," Peg said. "There's talk of the bank being shaky."

Heinz said nothing. Kim did not guess what was in the man's mind until he reached the table. Without a word he picked up the shoe box, snapped the cord that was tied around it, and, jerking the lid off, upset the box. Bundles of greenbacks fell on the table, more greenbacks than Kim had ever seen in his life before.

Yuma Bill cried out, a wild incoherent sound,

and grabbed for his gun. Heinz, expecting that, wheeled and struck him, a brutal blow that sent the little man crashing against the wall. His feet slid out from under him and he sat down, glassy-eyed. Stooping, Heinz pulled Yuma Bill's gun and threw it on the table.

Kim was caught off guard. It seemed senseless, so senseless that he was momentarily stunned by it. Then a wild rage was in him. He lunged at Heinz, his left fist swinging to the man's wide jaw. Heinz went down, falling hard.

"No, stop it!" Peg screamed, but neither man heard. Heinz rolled, grabbing for his gun, but he was half dazed and a little slow. Kim jumped at him, a heel coming down on Heinz's wrist and bringing a yell of pain out of the foreman.

"Quit it, you fools!" Peg screamed again.

Kim stepped back. Heinz lifted himself to his hands and feet, and looked up. There was a wildness in his gray eyes, and a driving hatred.

"You've got your gun," Kim said quietly. "Get up and make your play."

But Peg was between them then. "No more of this," she ordered. "You understand? The Clawhammer has enough enemies without fighting among ourselves."

"His idea." Heinz got up, feeling of his injured wrist. "It's time we found out who's running this outfit."

"It's past time you found out!" Peg cried

furiously. "I'm running it, and I tell you I won't have this brawling."

"Then fire him!" Heinz bellowed. "He's drawing good wages for nothing."

"I still need him," Peg said, her voice ominously low. "You've got a good job, Dutch. Do you want it or not?"

For a moment Heinz said nothing. He stood with his head dropped forward on his great shoulders, his breath sawing into the quiet.

"Yeah, I want to keep it," he said then, "which same you know, but you don't seem to know you're making a plumb bad mistake. Your dad wouldn't have made no such mistake."

Peg stepped forward, and for a moment Kim thought she was going to strike Heinz. She said, her voice controlled: "I'm not my dad. Why aren't you with the crew?"

Heinz ignored the question. He motioned toward the money.

"Use your head, Peg. Look at that. All the *dinero* you need to pay off every debt you owe. What difference does it make about Bonham and his bank? This is here for the taking."

Peg glanced at Kim, biting her lower lip and saying nothing. Yuma Bill was on his feet now, a hand raised to his face where Heinz had hit him.

"I suppose I was brought here so you could steal my money," he said bitterly. "That right, Logan?"

"No," Kim said.

But Heinz had eyes for no one but Peg.

"Bonham couldn't trace it," he urged. "Nobody could. Take it in the first thing in the morning and pick up them notes. I'll fix it so nobody will ever see the old man again." He motioned toward Yuma Bill. "And if Logan thinks as much of the Clawhammer as you allow, he won't squawk."

For a moment there was silence except for the metallic hammering of a clock on a corner shelf. Kim, too, was watching Peg. For that moment it seemed to him she was being tempted by what Heinz had said.

Then she said: "No! Get back to where you belong, Dutch."

Heinz took a long breath and shook his head as if this was beyond his comprehension. He moved to the door, then turned, cuffing his hat, and gave Kim a straight look. "I'll kill you, Logan," he said. "That's a promise."

"Shorty Avis said you'd been up there telling him to get out of the country. That his idea, Peg?"

"Tell him, Peg," Heinz said. "Tell him, or I will."

"No, it wasn't my idea," Peg said quickly. "I won't ask you again, Dutch. Get back to the crew."

Heinz's meaty lips fell apart. "Why, you . . ." He stopped as if reading something in Peg's face. Then he said heavily: "All right. Play it your way." He tramped across the living room and left the house.

Peg said nothing until the beat of hoofs came

clearly to them. Then she nodded at Yuma Bill.

"I'm sorry this happened," she said, "but there's no use apologizing for it now. You go get some sleep. I'll have breakfast for you before sunup. You'll get to town before the bank opens. And, Kim, you come back in. I want to talk to you."

V

In the bunkhouse the old chore man, Limpy, was pulling off his boots when Kim and Yuma Bill came in. He looked up, started to say something, and closed his mouth when he saw their bleak faces.

"Get your sleep," Kim said curtly. "We'll dust out of here afore sunup."

"This is a fine thing you fetched me into, Logan," Yuma Bill said.

"I know," Kim said, "I know." He left the bunkhouse.

When Kim returned to the house, Peg had moved the lamp from the kitchen to the big oak table in the living room. She was not in sight, but she called: "Sit down, Kim! I'll just be a minute."

He walked around the room, too restless to sit down. He stood for a moment in front of the picture of Sam Cody, Peg's father. Its gilt heavy frame was ornately carved. Somehow the fancy frame did not seem to fit the heavy-featured, boldly arrogant face. Even the eyes were insolent. They glared at Kim from under bushy brows as if resenting Kim's presence in the house.

A pusher, Kim had been told, a driver who slammed through to whatever he wanted, regardless of anybody who was in his way. Dutch Heinz had worked for him, and he had, Kim thought, learned his methods from old Sam. But Peg didn't even look like him. She was fighting for the Clawhammer's life, but her ways were not the ways of her father.

Kim did not know Peg had come up behind him until she said: "You think I look like him?"

He turned, catching the rich smell of a French perfume Fred Galt had recently put on the shelf of his Mercantile in Ganado. She had changed from her riding skirt and blouse to a blue dress with a tight-fitting bodice, a dress designed to make a man instantly aware that she was a woman, and appealing.

"No," Kim said. "You don't look like him at all."

"Why not?"

He let her see his admiration. This was the side of her that he liked; he did not like the side that made her wear mannish clothes and ride on roundup when she could have hired another hand.

Kim motioned to the picture. "He looks like a tough hand. Kind of a bull with his mind made up."

Peg laughed. "He was, all right. He drove a herd into the valley a long time ago. It was just after the mining boom was tapering off, and there were a few ranchers along the creek who didn't take to being pushed." She stopped, her eyes thoughtful. "But they got pushed just the same. He was a fighting man, Kim, and a good one."

"There's fighting men, and then there's fighting men," he said. "I don't reckon your dad and me would have hitched."

"Why?"

"I don't like anybody who ain't willing to live and let live," he said bluntly. "The ten-cow outfits like Shorty Avis's have a right to make out without somebody pushing 'em out of the country."

She sat down on the leather couch, smoothing her dress over her knees.

"I don't see it that way, Kim. If they aren't big enough and tough enough to hold what they've got, they won't last."

"They'll last if they're let alone."

She shook her head. "But they won't be let alone. The world I see is made for big people, so I aim to be big, so big that all the valley will be mine. It's not just money I want. It's prestige. I'll have it, Kim. You'll see."

"What about the Avises?"

"Right now I don't need the mesa range. Maybe I will tomorrow. If I do, they'll go." She gave him a close look. "Why are you interested in them? Is it the girl?"

He shook his head. "I just cotton to folks who don't run easy."

"Sit down." She patted the leather seat. "I was wondering if I should be jealous."

"No reason for you to be jealous of anybody." He dropped down beside her. "Looks like I'll be drawing my time in a day or two."

She laid a hand over his. "Kim, you wouldn't pull out when the ship's sinking, would you?"

"No place for me here. Not if Heinz stays."

"Don't get your neck bowed." She squeezed his hand. "I have some virtues along with my faults. Being loyal is one of them. Dutch was a kid wrangler when Dad came to the valley. He knows the cattle business, and I owe him a job if he wants it. If he doesn't, you're in line."

"Not me," he said quickly. "Not if it means pushing folks like the Avises."

"You aren't being smart." She drew her hand back. "None of these little outfits is worth us quarreling over. They'll never be anything but what they are."

"They've got the right to try," he said hotly. "Or just stay like they are if that's the way they want it."

She leaned back. "Kim, I need you. It's a funny thing how much you've done for me without actually doing anything. Hank Dunning is a lot like Dad was. He goes after what he wants. If you hadn't come, he'd have us backed against the wall by now."

"I've played my string out unless I do something," he said.

"I don't think so."

"I know so. It's smash or get smashed. Tomorrow we save the bank. Dunning won't like it. He'll move, and you'll need every man you've got."

She closed her eyes. "Kim, listen to me. I'm ambitious. You know that, but you don't know how I've laid awake nights, dreaming about what I'm going to do and thinking about where Dad made his mistakes. A bad winter and low beef prices almost ruined the Clawhammer. I suppose it was worry that killed him. Well, I'm not going to make his mistakes, but I'm a woman, so I'll use the weapons given a woman." She laughed, and faced him, her eyes bright. "Dutch is one weapon. You're another."

"I ain't so sure about me," he said roughly. "You've got use for me next week. Or next month. By that time Dunning will be dead or you'll be licked. Either way, you won't need me after that."

"I'll always need you, Kim."

She got up and walked across the room, her back to him, her skirt making a tight fit across her hips. She reached the table and, turning, raised her eyes to him. She ruffled the pages of a mail order catalogue in front of her, then pushed it away.

"You believe that, don't you?" she asked in a voice that was close to pleading.

"No. You need somebody. It don't have to be me."

"It's got to be you," she said quietly, "but there are times when I don't understand you. Then it seems you're almost a stranger."

"I get the same notion about you."

"Oh, I don't have many secrets, Kim."

"You do in your head," he told her.

She came back and sat down again beside him. "I've told you the only secret I have. It's why I mortgaged everything to Brit Bonham, hoping to put the Clawhammer back to where it was before Dad lost so much. It's why I hired you. It's why I do everything I do." She leaned back, hands laced over her knees, long legs swinging. "I'm going a long ways, Kim, but I have one fear. Maybe I'll be alone when I get there."

For some reason Kim thought of what Rocky Avis had said that noon about Peg being greedy, about him being a snake stomper without a dollar in his pocket.

"I don't savvy," he said finally. "Not exactly, but I know one thing. A gunslinger ain't fit to go along to where you're headed."

"Depends on the gunslinger. Why do you think I hired you?"

"Don't know."

"It's simple, Kim. You aren't like most of the

101

grub-line riders who come through here. I've always prided myself on my knowledge and judgment of men. I didn't make a mistake in you."

He looked at her curiously. "How am I different?"

"I mean . . . well, like insisting on taking the crew across the creek to finish Dunning. Most men who had a good thing would follow my orders and be satisfied."

"I've got my notions about how to do a job," he said.

"I know," she said softly. "You have a good many notions, Kim, strong ones. I can't help wondering. Tell me about yourself. Who your folks were and where they came from and everything."

"Nothing to tell. I was born in Missouri. Folks moved out to New Mexico and my ma died there. My dad died a couple of years later. I threw in with a salty bunch when I was sixteen. Been riding ever since till I got here."

"What was your mother like?"

"I don't remember her very well," he said. It was one thing he would not talk about.

"I don't remember much about my mother, either," she said. "She had red hair like mine, and I do remember terrific quarrels, but my mother and father were terribly in love with each other." She laughed. "We'd quarrel, too, wouldn't we?"

She was leaning toward him, her face close to

his, her red lips lightly parted. He put his arm around her and, drawing her to him, kissed her. In that instant she became a living flame in his arms, holding him, her lips clinging.

When she drew away, her hands caressed his cheeks.

"Kim . . . Kim," she murmured, "you were so slow. I'm getting pretty old, you know. Twenty-three. Almost an old maid."

"You're talking crazy," he said. "A little encouragement would bring any man in the valley walking to you on his knees. Even Hank Dunning, I reckon, if you wanted him."

She straightened, suddenly tense. "Kim, are you out of your mind?"

"Maybe. Kissing you would put any man out of his mind." He rose, looking down at her slim body, her lips that were smiling again. "I can't ask you to marry me. Not yet."

"Why?" she demanded. "Don't tell me you never thought about it."

"I've thought about it, all right." He paused, wondering what had happened to him. This was what he had wanted, a pretty wife and a big spread. But now that the opportunity was here, he could not take it. "Just seems like I've got to bring something to you besides my hands and a gun."

She looked at him, her face grave, then shook her head. "Don't make a mistake, Kim. Our life wouldn't be all sweetness and sunshine, but there would be other things to make up for it."

"Maybe I'm thinking about Dutch Heinz," he said. "Or maybe it's that I don't want to be Mister Peg Cody."

He left the house, leaving her frowning as if she were deeply troubled. He walked slowly toward the bunkhouse, wondering how big a fool he had been. If he had asked her to marry him, she would have said yes. He was sure of that. But he had not asked her, and the right moment might never come again.

Suddenly Kim was aware of the smell of a cigarette; he saw the bright tip glowing in the darkness. He reached for his gun, drew back his hand at once, realizing that an enemy would not give his presence away so carelessly.

"Well?" he said.

"Waiting," Yuma Bill said. "Just waiting. I ain't of a mind to trust anybody after what happened tonight."

"Are you making out you can't trust me?" Kim said angrily.

"No, I ain't," the little man said. "I was kind of dozing after Heinz cracked me, but I got the notion you sort of whittled him down to size."

"Well, why aren't you sleeping?"

"Why, it's just a matter of arithmetic. Anyway I count, you still add up to just one man, so I'll stay awake till this *dinero* is in Brit's safe."

"It'll be there by nine in the morning."

They walked on toward the bunkhouse.

Then Yuma Bill said: "She's playing with you, boy."

Kim gripped the little man's arm. "You pussy-footing window peeper. I oughta . . ."

Yuma Bill jerked away, angry. "I ain't no window peeper. I just knew how she'd perform. You think you're goin' to marry her, don't you? Sweet as the bottom of the sugar bowl, wasn't she?"

"Yeah, sweet enough," Kim said. "But I don't know about marrying her. Maybe I'll never have another chance."

"Then you'll be lucky. If you let her, she'll use you and drop you when she's done with you. I know because I've been through the mill."

"Women ain't all alike. Just because . . ."

"Her kind are. I can read her brand easy as I could the Clawhammer iron on a steer. She's thinking first, last, and always of Peg Cody, and she'll never change. You'll see."

"You're too suspicious," Kim muttered, and went into the bunkhouse.

But he did not sleep for a long time. He lay staring at the dark ceiling, more discontented with his life than he had ever been before. In spite of himself, he mentally compared Rocky Avis, sarcastic and sharp-tongued and at times cruelly honest, with Peg, and it surprised him that Peg was not flattered by that comparison. Still, he understood her as he had never understood her before, and he could not doubt the truth of what she had told him about herself.

VI

Breakfast was eaten by lamplight. Peg was silent and oddly aloof, her shoulders slack with weariness as if she had not slept. Only now and then did her eyes brush Kim's face, and they told him nothing.

When they finished eating, Yuma Bill rose, the shoe box under his arm.

"Thank you, ma'am," he said. "I hope my coming will be of some help to you as well as Brit."

"You're saving the Clawhammer," she said simply. "I'm the one who's doing the thanking."

Kim got up. "Time to go. I oughta be back a little after noon. Then I'll stay here unless you change your mind about hitting Dunning before he hits you."

"I'm not changing my mind, Kim," she said wearily, "but there's one thing I want you to do. Feeling against the bank was running pretty high yesterday. Dunning has convinced most people that Bonham's finished and we're to blame because the bank loaned us so much."

"That's why he'll be so mad when his scheme misses. He'll come hightailing out here with his outfit."

Peg waved his words aside. "I'll take care of him. Right now your job is to save the bank. If you take Yuma Bill into town, you'll probably both get killed before the money gets to Bonham, so I want you to leave Yuma outside of Ganado while you ride in and look things over. He could stay at Salty Smith's cabin."

"I'm supposed to be bullet bait. That it?"

"It'll be Dunning who gets the bullet if I know you," she said.

"Thanks for your confidence in my shooting eye, but . . ."

"She's right," Yuma Bill said. "It'd sure be bad to get to town and have something happen so Brit didn't get the *dinero*."

Kim shrugged. "We'll play it that way, if you want to, but I ain't sure it's the smart way. I'd like to know you trust my judgment."

"I trust your judgment, but I'm still giving the orders."

"And you'll always give them," he said angrily.

For a moment they faced each other, their wills clashing, and he sensed it would always be that way with them. Turning, he walked out of the house into the growing light. The air was cool and heavy with dampness. It would rain again that day.

Kim and Yuma Bill saddled by the murky light of a lantern, and, when they rode past the house, Peg stood silhouetted in the doorway. A chill of sudden fear ran down Kim's spine as he thought this might be the last time he would see her. He lifted a hand and she waved back. Then he rode on.

They splashed across Ganado Creek, and followed the road toward Ganado. The sun had tipped up over the Continental Divide, its scarlet light touching the Dragon Peaks across the valley. Slowly it climbed higher until it had rolled back the last of the shadows and full daylight was upon them.

Neither spoke for a time. Then Yuma Bill said: "Good grass."

"Cow paradise," Kim said. "Too bad anybody has to fight over it."

"Who's to blame?"

Kim shrugged. "I ain't paid to pass judgment, but, if I was, I'd say old Sam Cody. Peg's trying to hold what he left her."

"You'll find the blood of little men on every range like this," Yuma Bill said somberly. "And sooner or later you'll find the blood of more little men like Shorty Avis on the mesa. Greed begets greed. You're on the wrong side, boy."

"There's no right side," Kim said.

They rode in silence again. Once Kim hipped around in his saddle and looked to the series of benches that rose, step-like, toward the slick rock rim that swung in a wide circle around the east of the valley. Somewhere below that rim was Shorty Avis and his handful of cows, living in fear of Dutch Heinz's return.

Kim thought of Rocky and what she had done for him and Yuma Bill the day before. He glanced at the little man's weathered face as he thought of his words: *You'll find the blood of more little men like Shorty Avis on the mesa.* And discontent became a burning bitterness in Kim Logan.

"You hear anybody ride out last night?" Yuma asked suddenly.

"No. Why?"

"I did."

"You were dreaming. Nobody around but Peg."

Yuma Bill nodded. "That's just what I was thinking."

"But she wouldn't . . ." Kim stopped. The little man was staring at the willow-lined, twisting course of Pass Creek, his leathery face thoughtful. "Maybe she couldn't sleep and took a ride."

"She don't make a habit of it, does she?"

"No." Shrugging, Kim pointed to the cluster of buildings ahead of them. "That's Ganado yonder."

Yuma Bill lifted himself in his stirrups, staring at the town. A church spire pointed skyward; a weathered brick building stood to the right of the church.

"What's that brick building?" Yuma asked.

"Courthouse. Ganado is half cow town and half ghost town. The mining boom made it, and the old-timers figured they'd have the biggest city in Colorado, so they built a courthouse that'd be fit and proper."

"Mines wear out?"

Kim nodded. "Nothing lasts, I reckon."

"Some things do. You just ain't found 'em yet."

"Preaching again," Kim said irritably.

Yuma Bill shook his head. "Just talking." His craggy face softened as a grin worked across his mouth. "I was the same when I was your age, full of sass and vinegar and never thinking past the next glass of whiskey or the next gal I was goin' to kiss. Them things don't last."

"What does?"

"No use me telling you. Every man has got to find 'em out for hisself." He swung a hand in a sweeping gesture. "I can't help wondering why you don't get your own outfit. More grass here than two outfits can use. Or if there ain't, go back where Avis is. He's up purty high, but there's plenty of range."

"That would have been a good idea twenty years ago, when a man with a rope and a running iron could get a start, but folks kind of frown on them antics now."

"You can borrow."

"Where?"

"From the bank."

"And everything I'd made would go to Bonham for interest." Kim shook his head. "I never thought much about it until I got here with ten dollars in my pocket. Then I got to thinking. That started me to saving. First time in my life, but it's mighty slow."

"How much you got?"

"A little over a thousand."

Yuma Bill nodded, apparently surprised. "Let's swing over to the cabin," he said. "I'll wait out here for half an hour or so. If you don't come shagging back, I'll trail along into town."

They could see the cabin now, on the bank of the creek. As they reined toward it, Kim said: "I don't cotton to this idea much, even if it is Peg's."

"Just one reason I do. It's to her interest that we get this *dinero* to the bank."

When they reached the cabin, Kim's eyes searched the willows that crowded the creek.

"Looks like Salty's gone," he said. "If he ain't in town, he's usually fishing."

"Who is he?"

"An old Civil War vet. Been here for years. Made one of the first strikes and lost everything over a poker table. Now he's just waiting to die." Kim stepped down. "I'll see if he's inside."

There was no answer to Kim's knock. He pushed the door open and looked in. The cabin was empty.

"You can go in if you want to. Smith wouldn't care. Right friendly old cuss when he ain't drunk, but he ain't what you'd call clean. The air's better out here."

"I'd just as soon sit in the willows." Yuma Bill glanced at his watch. "Getting along toward nine. You hightail into town and take this box to the bank. Dunning'll be looking for me. He won't figure on you having it."

"I don't like the idea. I said I'd deliver you and your . . ."

Yuma Bill made an impatient gesture toward town. "Go on now. There's forty thousand in that box. I'm packing another ten in my money belt. I aimed to give all of it to Brit, but, coming across the grass just now, I got a sudden hankering to go into the cattle business." He winked. "With a hairpin named Kim Logan."

Kim's mouth sagged open. "Why, you . . ."

Yuma Bill laughed. "Pull your eyes back inside your head. You dust along. We'll be needing that bank one of these days, you and me."

"You know what we'll be into?" Kim demanded. "We'll be fighting Peg and Dunning both."

"All right. We'll fight 'em. Don't strike me you're the kind of huckleberry who'd be afraid."

"I ain't. I just didn't figure you'd want to buy a war of your own."

"I've bought one already. So have you. Let's say I want to sow some good seeds. Been a lot of weeds planted in these parts. Now take this box and move, or hod dang it, you'll be too late."

Shrugging, Kim took the box and got into the saddle. "Keep your eyes peeled," he advised.

Kim left the little man sitting his saddle in front of the cabin, his weathered face thoughtful. As Kim rode away, he wondered what sort of past Yuma Bill had that had molded him into the kind of man who would travel halfway across the state with a fortune in a shoe box, his sole purpose that of repaying an old debt to a banker who had once helped him.

Ganado lay just ahead, its false-fronted business buildings crowding Main Street, many of them deserted now, and dwellings decorated with gingerbread and carved bargeboards and surrounded by picket fences with carved corner posts. Most of the houses were empty; all were weathered to a dingy gray, their paint long gone. The fences needed repair, and the bulk of the boardwalks were splintered and grown up with weeds. A sort of genteel decay lay upon the town as if it had one eye upon its splendid past, the other closed to the future.

Kim had reached Main Street when Rocky Avis appeared from a livery stable and rode toward him. She brought her horse to a gallop, waving at him to hurry.

When he came alongside her, she cried: "You're mighty slow! Where's Yuma Bill?"

"He's laying low at Smith's cabin till I see how things stack up. I've got his box."

"Then get a move on. It's almost time for Brit to open up, and there's a line waiting."

"Then they're goin' to get a surprise. Come on and help me laugh in their faces."

Kim cracked steel to his buckskin and swept on down the street to the bank. He reined up and tied, his eyes sweeping the line of grim-faced men. Some were little ranchers from Dunning's side of the valley, the small fry dependent upon the HD just as Shorty and his neighbors were dependent upon the Clawhammer.

It was the others who brought a quick blaze of temper to Kim, townsmen who had no part in the feud, men who should be supporting Bonham— Doc Frazee, Fred Galt who owned the Mercantile, Luke Haines, the barber, and a dozen more. Sheriff Ed Lane was in the line, a bald man who gave Kim a small nod, tongued his quid to the other side of his mouth, and turned his eyes away.

"What you boys doing here?" Kim demanded.

"What does it look like?" Galt asked.

"Waiting for breakfast," Kim jeered.

"Why don't you go home and eat?"

Doc Frazee, wearing a Prince Albert that had once been black and now was faded to a sort of dingy green, glared at Kim. "We'll go home when we get our money, and don't think you can stop us. Bonham wouldn't have got in this fix if he

114

hadn't loaned our money to the Clawhammer."

"That's right!" Luke Haines cried in a shrill voice. "Just 'cause you're a tough hand working for the Clawhammer don't mean you can change our minds."

Galt, the first man in the line, looked at his watch. He was a nervous man given to stomach trouble. Now he shoved his watch back into his pocket and began pounding on the door.

"Nine o'clock, Bonham. Open up! Open up!"

Others crowded against Galt, adding their voices to his until the words—"Open up . . . open up!"—became a sullen, threatening rumble.

Kim could have showed them the money in the box. He could have said there was plenty to pay them and more, but he did neither. This was a selfish, senseless thing, a crime being committed by common men who thought they had their share of ordinary decency. It might have been forgivable in a man like Hank Dunning who pretended to be no better than he was; it was not forgivable in these townsmen.

Drawing his gun, Kim fired a shot over their heads. They faced him, bitter, sullen men who had been swept by hysteria past the point where they were capable of honest reasoning.

"Do that again, Logan," the sheriff bawled, "and I'll throw you into the jug for disturbing the peace!"

"Try it, Ed," Kim invited.

Lane looked away, jaws working steadily on his quid, a politician who had carried the star for ten years because he was master at bowing to the right man. After Sam Cody had died, Dunning had been the man. It was common gossip on Pass Creek that every HD man had voted five times at the last election.

"What's the matter with you?" Galt demanded. "This ain't none of your put in."

"Now maybe it is," Kim said. "I've got some money in this bank, maybe more than most of you boys, but I ain't asking for it. I figure the bank's sound."

"I don't," Galt flung back. "I ain't taking any chances."

"Are you trying to bust Bonham?"

"All I want is my *dinero*," Galt said doggedly.

"And you'll get it because you're first in line," Kim said, "but you don't give a hoot about the boys behind you. You're a two-bit, selfish, stingy, money-loving son."

There was a crowding up from the tail of the line, men ramming and elbowing as their voices rose in a menacing roar. Galt threw a quick look behind him, and his wizened face flooded with sudden fear.

Lane, the fourth man in the line, drew his gun and waved it at the ones behind him. "Order now, boys. Keep your places. Every man will have his turn."

"What time did you get here this morning, Fred?" Kim asked.

"None of your damned business!" the store man screamed.

"He was here at dawn," said a rancher far back in the line. "We had to do chores and had to ride in after that, so we couldn't get here that soon."

"Logan's just fixing to make trouble, Ed," Luke Haines said bitterly. "Run him in."

But Lane stood motionlessly, his eyes pinned on something down the street. Kim laughed, a contemptuous sound that ripped the last shred of dignity from the man.

"You poor fools!" he flung at them. "You're doing Dunning's dirty work, and you ain't smart enough to know it." He looked back along the line, watching them stir and shift, boot heels scraping on the broken boards of the walk. He asked: "Where is Dunning?"

"Inside," Doc Frazee said. "Talking to Bonham."

"Listen now, you chuckle-heads!" Kim shouted, "This ain't just my fight. Or the Clawhammer's. It belongs to all of you. You've bowed and scraped to Dunning until you've forgotten you were men. You'll get your money if you want it, but you don't need it, and, when you see that the bank's safe, you'll beg Bonham to take it back."

But they only stared at him defiantly, saying nothing, the men in the back of the line still pressing forward so that those in front were jammed hard against the door.

"I want to look at your ugly mugs in about ten minutes," Kim went on. "If you're worth anything, you'll get down on your knees to Brit Bonham. Then you'll go tell Dunning to crawl under a rock where he belongs!"

VII

Without another word, Kim bulled his way through the line, knocking Luke Haines flat on his face, and stalked around the corner to the back door of the bank. It was locked. He looked through the window, saw Bonham sitting at his desk, head bowed. Dunning sat across from him, his hawk-nosed face barren of expression.

Kim tapped on the window. When Bonham turned to look at him, he shouted: "Let me in, Brit! I've got something for you."

Bonham jumped up. Dunning said something, but Bonham shook his head and, running to the door, turned the key and pulled the door open. Kim stepped in, his eyes locking with Dunning's.

"Hank," he said, "I've waited a long time for this. You're licked."

Dunning rose. He was a tall man, taller even than Kim, and he seemed to be looking down right

118

confident. Casually he scratched his great beak of a nose.

"I reckon not, Logan," he said.

Kim walked to the desk and laid the box down. On the scarred walnut were Peg Cody's notes. Bonham dropped into his chair, his faded eyes on Kim's face.

"Did you see Yuma Bill?" he asked hoarsely.

"I saw him." Kim slashed the cord around the box. "Brit, I've learned more about human nature since I met Yuma Bill than I'd learned in ten years before. It takes a pretty good man to have a friend like him." Kim lifted the lid from the box. "Better open up, Brit. There's a few boys outside who seem to want some cash money."

Bonham cried out, a strained, hoarse sound, grabbed the box, and ran out of his office into the bank, shouting: "Charlie, open up! We'll pay 'em right down to the last nickel!"

Kim backed away from Dunning, hoping that this would be the moment he had long sought when Hank Dunning would go for his gun. Dunning only brushed at a lock of rebellious hair, his dark eyes probing Kim with cool insolence. Kim had never seen him excited. Now Dunning said deliberately: "Still lucky, Logan."

"Yesterday you sent Phil Martin and some of your boys across the creek after me. I reckon that opens the ball, don't it?"

Dunning shook his head. "Not today it don't."

"I don't cotton to playing coyote to your hounds. Let's finish it."

Again Dunning shook his head. "I never swap smoke with a hired hand." He walked past Kim and went into the back alley.

Kim stood staring after the big man until he disappeared around the corner. Then he followed Bonham into the bank.

The teller, old Charlie Bemis, had unlocked the front door, but was unable to get it open, so tightly were the men in front jammed against it. When he did, Fred Galt sprawled on his face, jumped up, and lunged across the room to the teller's wicket.

"I'm cleaning out my deposit!" Galt yelled. "Every cent. You hear, Bonham?"

"I hear quite well, Fred," the banker said as casually as if this were an ordinary occasion. "You'll get every cent as soon as Charlie looks up your balance."

Galt stood leaning against the counter, his bulging eyes fixed on the piles of currency stacked on a table beyond the teller's wicket. Others peered over his shoulder—Doc Frazee, Luke Haines, and the rest, men so stunned they were incapable of speech.

Then Haines let out a shrill squall. "Why, he's got enough *dinero* on that table to buy the Denver mint! Look at it, Fred."

The men stormed forward, trying to get a closer look at this money they had not believed was here, shoving and cursing. Smaller men were pushed back. A rancher cried out in pain, screaming for somebody to get off his corns. The sheriff got an elbow against his stomach that knocked his wind out of him. He reeled away and fell slackly against the wall, struggling for breath.

Charlie Bemis called: "Fred's got a balance of three thousand, two hundred and ninety-eight dollars, and fifty-two cents!"

"Be sure he gets that fifty-two cents," Kim said contemptuously.

"I certainly will." Bonham counted out Galt's money. "There you are, Fred. Three thousand and two hundred." He dipped into a drawer. "I'll let you have the rest in gold and silver, except the two pennies."

"Two-Penny Galt," Kim jeered.

"Say, that's a good handle for him." Rushmore, a rancher, slapped his leg, roaring with laughter. "Two-Penny! Yes, sir, that sure fits Galt."

Red-faced, Galt scooped up his money and pushed his way through the crowd. "Don't call me that, Rushmore, or I'll cut off your credit."

The rancher thumbed his nose at Galt. "We've needed a new store for a long time in this burg, Two-Penny."

"What are you goin' to do with that *dinero*, Two-Penny?" Kim demanded. "Lock it up in that cracker box of a safe of yours?"

Galt fled. Doc Frazee was staring at the

currency through the teller's window, his bony face thoughtful. "Boys," he said, "where'd we get the notion this bank wasn't sound?"

"Dunning," Rushmore said. "He passed the word out that we had to be here today and ask for our money, or we'd have a hard time hanging on to our spreads."

"Tell 'em, Brit," Kim said. "Go on. So they'll know what caliber Hank Dunning is."

Bonham straightened, his mouth working. "Peg Cody borrowed thirty thousand from me to restock the Clawhammer range. She's got five hundred head of prime steers she aims to sell in Durango this fall. That'll give her enough to pay the interest and take up a few of the notes. Dunning wanted them notes. He was in my office just now, offering me ten thousand for them."

"Why, the thieving crook!" Luke Haines spluttered. "He aimed to bust the Clawhammer."

"No doubt about it," Bonham said. "This bank is good. You boys ought to know that. I've got enough cash for ordinary business, but you'd have made me close my doors today if Kim hadn't fetched a chunk of money from a friend of mine. Now, if any of you want your deposits, you can sure have 'em. Just remember one thing. I don't want your business after today."

Doc Frazee pulled at his goatee, grinning like a boy caught in a cookie jar. "Well, Brit, I haven't got a good place to put my money if I had it.

Reckon I'll just leave it here where it'll be safe."

"Me, too!" Haines cried.

"You boys ought to go take a look at yourselves," Kim said. "I wish I had your pictures right now. They'd be handy to look at if you forget what kind of ears a jackass has got."

Doc Frazee felt of his, grinning. "Pretty long, ain't they?" He moved away from the window to where Kim stood. "Say, you and the HD boys must have had quite a tussle."

"Burned a little powder, all right," Kim said.

"They rode in late yesterday," Frazee said, "wanting me to patch 'em up and they sure needed it. Tonto Miles was the only one who didn't. Martin's got a busted left arm, and that young Ernie Deal got a slug in his brisket." Frazee lifted a bushy brow. "What started it?"

"They jumped us," Kim said shortly.

Frazee did not press the question. Shrugging, he turned away. "Well, Luke, let's see how your wife's making out. You'll be a father before noon, or I miss my guess."

The medico walked out, with Haines trailing behind him. The rest followed, abashed and silent. Bonham rubbed his face with trembling hands and dropped into a chair.

"Put the money in the safe, Charlie." He brought his gaze to Kim. "Where'd you leave Yuma?"

"At Smith's cabin. We stayed the night at the Clawhammer. When we left this morning, Peg allowed that Dunning might have a trap set up. She said for me to come in and see how things stacked up. Then Yuma got the notion I'd better fetch the box to you. Dunning wouldn't figure on me having it."

"He didn't," Bonham said. "Have any trouble yesterday?"

Kim told him what had happened, adding: "Brit, I've never been one to count on another man to pull my irons out of the fire. I didn't really figure Yuma Bill would be on that stage, but Peg said I'd better find out. Well, he was there, all right."

"I knew he'd be there unless something happened." The banker rose. "Come on back, Kim."

Bonham walked to his private office, a tired, stoop-shouldered old man. He sat down behind his desk, motioning for Kim to take the other chair. Picking up Peg's notes, he stacked them neatly.

"I've been here a long time," Bonham said. "I've seen this town boom and I've seen it rot. I had the first bank here, and the last. I could have been a rich man if I'd used my money like some did, but I always had the notion that I'd live longer and die happier if I mixed a little justice with the banking business." He made a gesture toward the street. "But look what it got me. Just let somebody start some talk and they want their money."

"Well, I guess you sowed the right seeds," Kim said, "or Yuma Bill wouldn't have been on that stage."

Bonham started to fill his pipe. "Yuma still talking about sowing seeds?"

Kim nodded. "I told him he oughta get a pulpit."

Bonham dribbled tobacco into his pipe and tamped it down. "No, he don't need a pulpit. You know, there was a time when he was the meanest, orneriest son of Cain who ever toted a gun. Now he's a different man. Call it a miracle, if you want to, or just come out and call me a liar, but I seen it happen."

Kim waited, watching the banker light his pipe and blow out great clouds of smoke. There was more to the story, but he saw that Bonham was not of a mind to tell it now. He motioned to the notes.

"How close did Dunning come to getting them?"

Bonham's eyes filled with misery. "So close that I'm ashamed of myself. It was that or go bust. After being in the banking business for thirty years . . . well, I was reaching for any straw I could see."

"It would have finished Peg," Kim said morosely. "I don't savvy it, Brit. Dunning don't strike me as being the kind of a hairpin who'd figure out a sneak deal like this."

Bonham puffed for a moment. Then he said, troubled: "There's something that ain't right, but I can't put my finger on it. Now old Sam was the sort who kicked everybody out of his way. He didn't have a friend in the valley except old Limpy and Dutch Heinz. When Sam was alive,

125

Dunning behaved. Then after Sam died, Dunning decided he'd start pushing."

Kim rose. "Well, might as well ride out and tell Yuma that everything's all right."

"I'll ride along." Bonham reached for his hat. "Been a long time since I saw old Yuma."

"Kim!" It was Rocky Avis. "Kim, you here?"

"He's talking to Brit," Charlie Bemis told her.

Kim wheeled out of Bonham's office. Rocky stood in front of the teller's window, her face paler than Kim had ever seen it.

"What's up?" he asked.

He had always thought of her as a steady, capable girl, the kind who belonged to this wild land in which she lived. Now he saw terror in her dark eyes; she was close to being hysterical.

"Tonto Miles." She gripped Kim's arms. "He's out in front talking to Ed Lane. He says he'll kill you the minute you come out of the bank."

A deep satisfaction filled Kim. It was Dunning he wanted, not Miles, but a fight with Miles might force Dunning.

"Tonto can try, Rocky," Kim said. "That's all."

"But Lane says he'll jail both of you if you start anything."

"If we're both alive." Kim shrugged. "Ed's just talking through his hat."

"He's Dunning's man. It's a trap! You can't go out there, Kim."

"Rocky's right," Bonham said. "Up till now

you've just been a gnat buzzing in Dunning's ear, but now that you've knocked the bottom out of his scheme, he's got to get you."

"I'll bring your horse around to the back," Rocky urged. "You've got to get out of town."

He shook his head, giving her a tight smile. "You know I can't do that."

"No sense getting yourself killed for nothing," Bonham said in exasperation. "Get back to the Clawhammer and fetch Heinz and his boys in. You're goin' to have a finish fight sooner or later."

"Peg don't see it like that," Kim said. "She says she hired my gun, and it's time I was earning my pay."

"Why, she knows . . ." Bonham stopped, suddenly thoughtful. "I wonder."

"What?"

Bonham shook his head. "Nothing. Just wool gathering."

Kim stepped away from Rocky and checked his gun. She moved in front of him, her small chin outthrust. Her fear was gone now. She was angry, with the same quick anger he had seen when she had bitterly called him a snake stomper. "Kim, do you think Peg Cody is the kind of woman a man should die for?" Rocky demanded.

"Why, I hadn't thought of it just that way."

"Then start thinking. I told you she was greedy."

"Well, we're all a little greedy, I reckon."

"But not like Peg Cody. Kim, you can't go out

there and get yourself killed just for her hundred dollars a month."

"It's for something a little more than that, Rocky."

"No, it isn't. Kim, can't you see how it is? There are some things that are worth dying for. I mean, things a man can believe in, but this is . . . is just throwing your life away for nothing."

He shook his head, looking down at her flaming face, and, oddly enough, he thought of her as being pretty. Not in the way Peg Cody was. More like the beauty of a mountain storm.

"I've got a job to do," he said.

"Let him go, Rocky," Bonham said.

Rocky whirled on him. "You men are all alike, but I thought you'd be different. He saved your bank for you. . . ."

Kim moved past her, his .44 riding easily in its holster, and walked out of the bank into the sunlight. He stopped for a moment, letting his eyes get used to the glare.

"Charlie," he heard Bonham say, "get them Winchesters out of the closet."

He knew then that he would have a fair fight, and that was all a man who lived by the gun could ask.

Tonto Miles stood in front of the Belle Union, a burly man who had come to the valley after Kim had.

"I've been looking for you, Logan!" he bawled.

Ed Lane, who had been standing beside Miles, drifted away and disappeared. Kim moved along the walk until he was clear of the hitch pole, then stepped into the street, hands at his sides. Neither Dunning nor Martin was in sight. There had been other men on the boardwalk. Now they were gone.

Miles stepped off the walk and moved into the street, his great head canted forward on massive shoulders. Suddenly—and it was the first time in Kim's life that he had ever felt this way—he was tired of fighting.

A few minutes before Dunning had said he never swapped smoke with a hired hand. Kim Logan was that. No more. No less. Here they were, Tonto Miles and Kim Logan, hired hands, both of them, although the hope was in Kim that he was more than that to Peg Cody. Their deaths would settle nothing. Other men would be hired. He thought of the fellow who had fallen off the rim the afternoon before, a man who had made a bad bargain. Then the thoughts fled. This was no time for them if he wanted to live.

VIII

Slowly Kim and Tonto Miles moved into the street, tense, watchful. One measured step, then another, boots falling into the street dirt. Overhead the sun was a brilliant searing ball in a clear sky, drawing moisture from a wet earth, the air heavy with the smell of it. A bird began to sing, a sweet, clear sound that beat against Kim's ears. It might be the prelude for his passage into eternity.

They were close, so close that Kim could see the purple veins in Miles's cheeks, the red flecks in his eyes. Then Miles made his draw. Warned by the down drop of the man's right shoulder, the quick flick of lips pulled tightly against yellow teeth, Kim drove his right hand toward gun butt and swept it clear of leather. It was a swift, sure motion without waste, the perfect co-ordination of nerve and muscle that comes only after long practice.

Powder flame made its brief stab of fire against the sun's glare. The roar of the shot ran along the street, deserted except for these two. Then Kim stood alone, staring down at Tonto Miles who lay with his face in the dirt, right hand flung out beside his unfired gun. A revulsion swept through him, a sickness, and with it a bitter hatred for Hank Dunning who had caused this.

Men boiled into the street, Doc Frazee in the lead, black bag in hand, the tails of his faded Prince Albert flying behind him. Kim saw Brit Bonham and Charlie Bemis standing in front of the bank, cocked Winchesters in their hands. Then he heard Frazee say: "Right through the heart. Never saw no better shooting."

Kim went into the saloon. He said—"Whiskey." —and only then was he aware that he still held his gun. He holstered it, eyeing the bartender who shoved a bottle and glass at him with the wariness of a man approaching a coiled rattlesnake. That was grimly familiar, but after all these years Kim still resented it.

They would remember him, these men who had watched from open doorways and windows, and they would be afraid of him. There had been a time when street fights were common in Ganado, but only a few like Doc Frazee and Brit Bonham would remember. There had long been talk of trouble between the Clawhammer and the HD; bets had been placed as to when the first blood would be spilled. Now the day had come, and from this hour Kim Logan would be a marked man.

He took his drink and set the glass back on the polished mahogany. He filled it again, staring moodily at the amber liquid. No good. Liquor could not take the sourness from him.

Men came in. The batwings slapped shut, and

Kim turned his head. Sheriff Ed Lane stood there, and Johnny Naylor, the shotgun guard, stood behind him. Both were scared and showed it, Naylor being so panicky he was close to bolting. Lane came on until he stood within ten feet of Kim. He said, trying to appear tough: "Lay your gun on the bar, Logan. You're under arrest."

For a moment Kim did not move. He stood with his left hand on the bar, his right within inches of gun butt, staring blankly at Lane. He said finally: "Say that over, Ed."

"You're under arrest," Lane repeated. "Put your gun on the bar and head for the door."

"You can't pull this off," Kim said. "A dozen men saw that fight. You know I couldn't duck it."

"I ain't arresting you for plugging Miles," Lane said, emboldened by Kim's lack of resistance. "It's for stopping the stage yesterday and taking a gent named Yuma Bill off it."

Kim's angry gaze swung to Johnny Naylor. "So you've sold out, too, Johnny. Your caliber is a sight smaller than I thought it was."

"I didn't sell out to nobody!" Naylor cried. "I just ain't goin' to let you get away with stoppin' the stage and takin' a man off at point of a gun. You ain't that big, Logan."

"I didn't take him. He got out when I mentioned Brit Bonham. Remember?"

"Yeah, and you had a gun in your hand. Remember that?"

132

Kim shrugged. "If I hadn't, you'd have drilled me. I had to keep you quiet so I could talk to Yuma."

"You held a gun on us," Naylor said doggedly. "You scared the devil out of us. That fat woman fainted. Might have died of heart failure. If we've got any law around here, it won't stand for it."

"We've got law all right," Lane said smugly, "and it don't stand for them kind of shenanigans. Now are you . . . ?"

"If I hadn't taken Yuma, some of Dunning's outfit would have. He'd have been beefed by now and the bank would be busted."

"He wouldn't have been touched," Naylor said with malicious triumph. "We rolled into Ganado without no more trouble."

Doubts struck Kim then. He had been so sure the stage had been stopped again he had not questioned it.

"You're lying, Johnny," he said.

"I ain't neither. Ask the driver. Or the passengers. The drummer's over at the hotel and that fat woman is Luke Haines's mother-in-law. She's in Luke's house now. Go ask her."

"All right," Kim said, "but you still haven't got a charge against me, Ed. We stopped at Rocky Avis's place on our way down and she cooked dinner for us. She'll tell you Yuma wasn't no prisoner. You can't make kidnapping out of it."

"I'm making it kidnapping, all right," Lane said

doggedly. "I'll ask Rocky, but I've got to throw you into the jug."

Ed Lane was a poor excuse for a lawman. Still, Kim could not draw a gun on him. Killing a man like Tonto Miles was one thing; shooting the sheriff was quite another. Kim laid his gun on the bar. He walked toward the batwings.

"I won't be in long, Johnny," he said. "Not when Yuma Bill tells his story. Then you'd better get out of my way."

"Take more'n that to get you out of the jug," Naylor said, his terror gone now that Kim's gun was not in his holster. "Butch said the Clawhammer wasn't big enough to save your hide."

"We'll see," Kim said, and pushed through the batwings.

Miles's body had been moved and the street was empty. Kim paused, wondering who would go to the Clawhammer for him. Peg, he was sure, would arrange for bail and get him out as soon as she heard.

"Keep moving," Lane said. "Try anything and I'll plug you."

Kim turned toward the courthouse, resentment smoldering in him. Lane did not need to keep the gun in his back, but it was like the man, now that Kim was unarmed. He would relish telling Dunning how he had arrested and disarmed Kim Logan who had killed Tonto Miles.

They passed Luke Haines's barbershop, Galt's

Mercantile, and, when they reached Doc Frazee's drug store, Kim heard running steps behind him. It was Rocky Avis and her temper was honed sharp again.

"Ed, what are you up to now?" Rocky demanded.

Lane licked brown-stained lips, eyeing Rocky warily. "Don't you try none of your tricks. You're a wildcat all right, but my jail can hold wildcats along with gunmen."

Rocky stamped a foot, so angry that Kim thought she was going to slap Lane.

"Why are you arresting him?"

"What's it to you?"

"Plenty. You put out some talk about arresting anybody who got into a gunfight in Ganado, but you can't make it stick, and you know it."

"I'll make this stick. He's arrested for kidnapping a feller named Yuma Bill. Now git back."

"Why, you pumpkin-headed fool! Yuma Bill wasn't kidnapped. They stopped at my place and I cooked dinner for them. I saw how it was."

"Johnny Naylor says different. Now git out of the way, Rocky, or so help me, I'll . . ."

"Johnny Naylor, is it? We'll see about that."

Rocky whirled and started back along the walk. "Rocky, wait!" Kim called. She turned back, standing motionlessly as if poised for flight. "Ride out to Clawhammer and tell Peg what happened. She'll get me out."

Rocky stared at him blankly for a moment, then

she flared: "You don't need your precious Peg. I'll fix this."

Again she whirled, and this time Kim let her go.

"She ain't so big," Lane said smugly. "Move along."

The brick courthouse, Ganado's chief reminder of the glory that was past, stood at the end of the block. Only the first story was used. The other two were empty, most of their windows knocked out by Ganado's stone-throwing boys. They had been boarded up, giving the building the same appearance of decay that was typical of the town.

Kim pulled the front door open. "Some oil would stop that squeak," he said, and went on down the dark hall to Lane's office, floorboards *squeaking* dismally under his feet.

The sheriff threw a cell door back and motioned with his head.

"Ain't had much business lately." Lane locked the door behind Kim. "Time it was picking up. A sheriff oughta earn his salary, hadn't he?"

"Yeah. Dunning's money."

Lane turned to spit in the direction of the big brass spittoon at the end of his desk. He swung back, wiping a hand across his mouth.

"Well, now, you go ahead and talk ornery if you want to. Won't make me mad. Won't do you no good, neither."

Kim sat down on the bunk and rolled a smoke, paying no attention to Lane who stood staring at him a little uncertainly, apparently surprised that Kim was taking the arrest so calmly.

"Hungry?" he asked.

"No."

Lane dropped Kim's gun into a drawer of his desk.

"I'll fetch you a meal from the hotel afore sundown," he said, and walked down the hall, the *squeak* of the boards coming back to Kim.

Kim had been in jail a few times, but never for more than an hour or so, and never for anything more serious than cracking some local cowboy on the nose during a Saturday night free-for-all. This could be serious. He smoked his cigarette down and rolled another, his hatred for Hank Dunning becoming a poison in him.

One thing was clear to Kim. Dunning was a more careful man than he had thought. He had rigged up one trap behind another so that, if the first failed, there would be the second, and then a third. He had not succeeded in buying Peg's notes, so he had tried to remove Kim by throwing a gunman at him. That had failed, but at least he had Kim in jail, and it was more than probable that he could swing enough influence to secure a conviction. Then he could move on the Clawhammer without fear of serious opposition.

Kim thought briefly of Rocky, wondering what she had in mind and having no real hope of her success. He should have asked Lane to send Brit

Bonham to see him. Bonham would see that Peg heard what had happened. Peg would get him out. She needed him. He had every reason to think she loved him. Then he swore and rubbed his cigarette out. He had missed a bet last night because of a perverse notion that he had to prove to Peg what he could do before he asked her to marry him.

He heard steps in the hall, the floor *squeaked,* and Kim got up from the cot and rattled the bars.

"Hey, you out there!" he yelled.

There was no answer, but the steps kept coming; the floorboards *squeaked* just outside the sheriff's office. Then the door opened. Lane came in, red-faced and sullen. Johnny Naylor was behind him, then Rocky Avis, and Naylor's wife, Della. Naylor looked like a kid who has just been soundly thrashed, Rocky was smiling, and Della had the appearance of a tornado with the cork pulled.

Without a word Lane unlocked the cell door and swung it back.

"You're free," he said sourly. "Naylor changed his story. Said the stage had already stopped and Yuma Bill got out 'cause he wanted to."

Kim walked out of the cell and, crossing to Lane's desk, opened a drawer and took out his gun. He checked it, and dropped it into holster, guessing that Della had pulled this off. She was Rocky's best friend, from one of the small ranches on the mesa.

"What are you waiting on?" Rocky asked. "You like it in here?"

Kim grinned. "Can't say I do, but I'm a mite curious."

"I'll settle your curiosity right now," Della said sharply. "It's going to take some regular Sunday school living from Johnny to make me forget this. If we can't get along on his wages . . ."

"Now, Della . . . ," Naylor began.

"Don't Della me," she flung at him. "I wouldn't blame Kim if he blew your head off, but I've got a hunch I'm saving your life by telling him what you did. He was sore about you stopping the stage, Kim. Maybe he had a right to be, but he didn't have a right to take Dunning's hundred dollars and swear you into jail. Now he's swearing you out."

"A hundred dollars, was it?" Kim asked softly. "You lie cheap, Johnny."

"I didn't do no lying," Naylor muttered. "You did have a gun in your fist."

"But you didn't think to tell Ed about it until after Tonto Miles cashed in. That right?"

"Yeah, it's right," Naylor said sulkily.

"And you knew that Miles was going to make a try for me?"

Naylor looked at Kim defiantly: "I knew all right. He was sore 'cause you shot the living daylights out of his bunch below the rim yesterday. Dunning claims you're fixing to pull this valley

139

into the blamedest range war the country ever saw. If it takes killing you to stop it, why, he thinks . . ."

"All right," Lane broke in. "No use of this palaver. Vamoose."

Della gripped Kim's arm. "Johnny got you into this," she said quickly, "but now he's got you out. You're not sore at him, are you?"

"I can take care of myself!" Naylor shouted, his pride outraged. "Del, you'd better stay out of all this!"

"I ain't sore," Kim said, and gave Della a sour grin. "Not much. Anyhow, you're too pretty to be a widow. . . . Come on, Rocky."

They went down the hall, Rocky half running to keep up with Kim's long strides.

"I knew Della would fix Johnny," she said. "She doesn't like Dunning any more than I do. When Johnny started bragging about the hundred dollars he'd won at poker, Del guessed what had happened and she made him tell her the truth."

"Wouldn't be hard to guess." Kim grinned. "Johnny's the worst poker player in the valley."

"Del tells him that," Rocky declared, "but Johnny doesn't think he's so bad. He keeps trying to show her that he's not as hopeless as she thinks he is."

They stepped into the sunlight. Kim took a deep breath.

"You know, Rocky," he said, "good air is

140

something you don't put the right price on till you're cooped up in a stuffy jail for a while."

"It's that way with a lot of things, I guess," she told him. "What are you going to do now?"

"Go back to the Clawhammer. Say, did Yuma Bill get into town?"

"Why, I don't know. I haven't seen him."

"Let's take a sashay out to Smith's cabin and see what's holding him up," Kim suggested. "You'll want to pick up your dad's horse he rode anyhow."

"Kim!" The girl gripped his arm. "Look!"

He stared down the street, shocked into silence by what he saw. Hank Dunning and Phil Martin were riding into town from the south. Smith's cabin was in that direction. Dunning was leading the black horse that Kim had borrowed from Shorty Avis for Yuma Bill. A man was lashed face down across the saddle.

Kim ran toward them, a terrible fear crowding him. Yuma Bill was dead! He was too far away to recognize the man tied in the saddle. He could not tell at this distance whether the man was dead, but he knew. He should never have left Yuma Bill alone.

IX

Now men were boiling into the street.

"Another killing!" someone shouted.

By the time Kim and Rocky reached Galt's Mercantile, Dunning and Martin had reined up in the middle of the street. Men crowded around them, asking questions, but Dunning ignored them. Kim shouldered through the crowd, his eyes making certain what had been in his mind. The man tied across the saddle was Yuma Bill, and he was dead.

Brit Bonham was beside Kim, shaking his shoulder. "It's Yuma Bill! It's Yuma Bill!"

Kim put his gaze on Dunning who was staring down at him, black eyes somber.

"You killed him, Dunning?" Kim asked.

Fury swelled the big man's chest. He swore, motioning to Ed Lane, behind Kim. "Hear that, Sheriff? This killing thief wants to know if I done it."

"Did you?" Kim asked hoarsely.

"Tell 'em what you saw, Phil," Dunning ordered.

Martin's left arm was in a sling. His broad face was gray, mirroring his suffering. His hand clutched the saddle horn as if it were an effort to remain upright.

"I was coming into town to have Doc look at my arm," Martin said slowly. "Logan and another *hombre* was riding in. They stopped at Smith's cabin. They got down and Logan opened the door. He looked in, then he turns around and shoots the other fellow. He grabs the dead man's money belt and lights out for town."

"It ain't often you've got an eye witness to a murder, Ed," Dunning said.

Kim stood motionless, stunned. He heard the sullen mutter of the crowd, heard Fred Galt shout: "That's why he was so high and mighty about us getting our money out of the bank! He already had his nest feathered."

"It's a lie!" Rocky cried. "I met Kim on the way to town this morning. . . ."

"But you didn't see him at Smith's cabin, did you?" Dunning demanded. "You didn't see 'em from the time they stopped at Smith's cabin till Logan left, did you?"

"No, but . . ."

"All right, Ed," Dunning said. "This girl don't know nothing about it. Phil does, because he saw it."

Kim stepped back, hand dropping to gun butt. It was a rigged play, smart and brutal, another trick lined up behind the others that had failed.

"Take it easy, Logan." Lane's gun rammed against Kim's back. "That cell you left is empty and waiting." He lifted Kim's .44. "Back you go."

"Hold on!" Kim shouted. "Martin's lying! This man was alive when I left him. If I'd aimed to kill him, I'd have taken the *dinero* I fetched to the bank, and I'd have kept going."

"No," Dunning said. "You're too smart for that. Bonham had told about a friend coming with some money. It's my guess you spent the night at the Clawhammer and Peg Cody knew what was in the box, but chances are she didn't know he was toting more *dinero* in his money belt. You could take that and figger you was safe 'cause no one knew he had it on him."

"I saw what I saw," Martin said doggedly. "I'll swear to it if this killing son lives long enough to be tried."

"He won't!" Galt bawled. "I'll donate the rope, and put the loop on his neck myself!"

Lane wheeled on the storekeeper, making a show of anger.

"None of that talk, Fred. I never lost a prisoner out of my jail yet, and I ain't starting with Logan."

Bonham had stood as if paralyzed. Only now did he seem to grasp what was happening. He gripped Lane's arm.

"Ed, if you used your noggin, you'd know Martin's lying. Logan's been in town since nine this morning. Martin wouldn't have waited all this time to tell what he saw."

"I tried to get to town," Martin said, "but I couldn't make it. Fainted, I reckon. Fell out of

144

my saddle. Hank found me." He stopped, swaying, and pitched to the ground.

"Doc!" Dunning called. "Take care of Phil."

Doc Frazee motioned to Galt and Johnny Naylor. "Tote Martin over to my office. Dunning, you take the body to my back room." His long face was dark with anger. "But there's one thing I want to say. When I first hit this here camp, it was plumb wild, but I never seen nothing like this for framing a man. It's too pat, Dunning, just too pat."

Frazee stalked across the street to his office.

"Move along, Logan," Lane said.

"Get word to Peg, will you, Brit?" Kim asked, and, when Bonham nodded, Kim winked at Rocky. "It's all right. I'll be out again by sundown. Ed's goin' to get plumb discouraged, locking me up."

Kim paced along to the courthouse, knowing it wasn't all right, not on a murder charge with Fred Galt hating him as he did, and Dunning willing to oil men's throats with free whiskey in the Belle Union. Nothing more was needed to start a blood-lusting mob toward the courthouse. Saner men like Brit Bonham and Doc Frazee would be pushed aside.

As Kim reached the courthouse, Lane asked: "Scared?"

"Some."

"You've got cause to be," Lane said with satisfaction.

They went in and on down the length of the dark hall. And for the second time that day the cell door banged shut behind Kim.

In the office a strange uneasiness possessed Ed Lane. He dropped Kim's gun into the same drawer and paced around, nervously chewing on his quid of tobacco. Finally he called: "Anything you want, Logan?"

"No."

"Hungry yet?"

"No."

"Ain't et since breakfast, have you?"

"No."

"I'll go over to the hotel and have 'em cook you up a good meal. Anything special you want?"

"What are you trying to do, ease your conscience by giving a condemned man his last meal?"

Lane bristled. "You won't get your last meal till after you're legally tried and convicted, which same you will be. And don't say nothing about my conscience. I didn't take an old man off the stage and then plug him."

"How come you didn't arrest Martin and his outfit for jumping me and Yuma Bill yesterday?"

"Nobody made no complaint," Lane said, turning sullen. "If I'd arrested anybody, it'd have been you, jumping 'em like you done."

"So that's the way Martin tells it. How did he account for being on the Clawhammer's side of the creek?"

"They wasn't breaking no law, just riding."

Lane wheeled and stamped out. Silence then, tight and oppressive. Kim sat down on his bunk and rolled a smoke. He fired it and took a long drag, but there seemed to be no taste to it. He ground it out, got up, and paced his cell, physically sick. In the few hours he had known Yuma Bill, he had learned to respect him as he had respected few men in his turbulent life.

Death was not new to Kim. Like most men who live by the gun, the knowledge that death is the natural and inevitable destiny for every human was never fully absent from his mind. But these last hours had changed him as surely as a dam diverts a flowing stream, and Yuma Bill had done the changing, Yuma Bill who would have made himself felt in the entire valley if he had lived. Now Kim was haunted by the thought that he was at least partly to blame for the little man's death.

Another thing, too, added to his misery. As far back as he could remember, he had wanted to own a ranch, a natural ambition for a man who had been raised in cattle country. Until he had come to Pass Creek Valley, he had never really planned beyond the next day. But here was a country big enough for a dozen ranches, although now there were just two with the threat of war between them. That threat had been largely responsible for keeping other cowmen out and

147

for holding the little outfits back on the poor graze of the mesa.

Then Yuma Bill had proposed a partnership. It had been right at his fingertips, what Kim wanted more than anything else. Now it was snatched away. He was back as a hired gun hand with $1,000 in the bank, accused of murdering the very man who had promised to turn a dream into reality.

Hours later, it seemed to Kim, Lane brought Brit Bonham to his cell. The banker was wearing a slicker.

"Rain's about here," he said.

Kim had not been aware of the gathering storm.

"Won't last long," he said, and watched Lane search Bonham for a gun, saying he wasn't taking any chances. He drifted back to his desk, giving Kim and Bonham a chance to talk. It was a courtesy Kim had not expected from him.

"I sent a man to the Clawhammer," Bonham said. "He oughta be back in another hour or so. If Peg's got any sense, she'll send her boys in and yank you out of here before it's too late."

"I won't run," Kim said sharply. "Running convicts a man if nothing else does."

"You can't prove your innocence locked up here," Bonham snapped. "Use your head, boy. Dunning's buying free drinks in the Belle Union. He's bent on getting rid of you, and a rope is a cheap way to do the job."

"Must be some men in town who don't figure the way he does," Kim said.

Bonham glanced at the sheriff and brought his eyes back to Kim.

"Sure. Me and Doc and Charlie Bemis. Maybe one or two more. Or supposing you stand trial? What chance have you got against Martin's testimony?" Bonham shook his head. "We've got to bust you out some way."

Kim gripped the bars. "I've been wondering about a couple of things. Was Dunning in town when Tonto Miles and I tangled?"

"Don't know. I'll find out."

"And what about old Salty Smith?"

"I've been wondering myself," Bonham said. "I don't think he's been around town today."

"Then he'd be fishing."

Bonham nodded, considering this. "He never fishes downstream. Usually he goes about a mile up the creek and fishes back down. Thick as them willows are, he could have been in sight of his cabin when it happened and seen the whole thing."

"He knows Dunning and Martin," Kim said. "If he saw it, he'd be afraid to talk."

"I'll ride out there. He'll talk to me." Bonham swung away from the bars.

"Done?" Lane asked.

"Yeah, except for one question, Ed. It's a pretty poor stick of a sheriff who don't think of justice first. You ain't goin' to be proud of yourself if you hang the wrong man."

"What're you getting at?"

"I've been wondering what you'd do if you had proof that Martin or Dunning shot Yuma Bill?"

Lane snorted. "I've got proof that Logan done it. That's all I need."

"A good lawman looks a little deeper than what's thrown on top for him to see. It's like Doc said. This thing is too pat."

"Makes sense," Lane said doggedly. "Anyhow, it's up to the jury, not me."

"Maybe it'll never go to a jury."

Lane chewed hard, his face turning red. "Brit, nobody's gonna take Logan out of here," he burst out. "You hear? Nobody."

"They'll try, and I can't see you being man enough to die bucking a lynch mob. There's another thing you'd better be thinking on. If Kim killed Yuma Bill, he done it before nine this morning. That right?"

"Yeah, but . . ."

"Doc says he hasn't been dead that long." Bonham turned back to Kim. "Your horse is in the stable. He'll be taken care of." He swung around and went out.

Lane stood motionlessly. Then he muttered—"*Aw,* Doc couldn't tell."—and stamped out after Bonham.

It began to rain with sudden violence, much as

the storm had come the day before. Kim stood up on his cot and looked out of the one small window. This was the shabbiest and most decayed part of a decaying town. Log cabins scattered haphazardly about, doors half off their hinges, roofs falling in, yards and streets grown high with weeds. Now, for one brief moment, the rain drew a silver curtain across this tawdry scene.

Kim got down, futility weighing heavily upon him. He had always been a man to depend upon himself and his gun, confident of his strength and speed. Now, for the first time that he could remember, he was completely trapped. There was no way out, no way by which he could help himself. There were those who wanted to help him, but if they did, they would risk their own lives, and that he did not want.

He rolled a cigarette and smoked it, seeing the situation with stark clarity. His one hope lay in old Salty Smith, but in spite of what Bonham had said, the hope at best was a slim one.

At first he had expected help from Peg. Now, with the slow minutes dragging by, he realized that Peg could not help him, that his trust in her was as empty of real value as a pocketful of fool's gold. Even if she should be willing to bring her crew down from the high country, Dutch Heinz would refuse to do anything.

Then a new fear clutched Kim. This might have been pulled off by Dunning to lure the

Clawhammer men away from the cattle and leave them unguarded. He pushed that thought from his mind at once. One thing overshadowed everything else in Peg's mind—the safety of her herd. She would not order her men to leave her cattle whether Kim Logan's neck was stretched or not.

The storm moved on. Thunder was softened by distance; the only lightning was that along the horizon. Kim knew how it would be outside—a hot clear sun, the heavy damp air, mud squishing under boot heels, the clean smell of a washed, steaming earth. Those were things that a free man could see and smell and feel.

A free man! Panicky, he jumped up and pounded the bars. He shouted and kicked, and then realizing what was happening to him, he dropped back on the cot, ashamed. He wasn't licked. A man had a chance as long as he was alive, but no one except Brit Bonham would gamble on that chance. Even Rocky Avis hadn't come to see him. Not that he blamed her. She had probably taken her father's black horse and headed for home. She had already done enough for him. More than enough. More than he had any right to expect.

He clenched his hands and spread them and clenched them again. He got up and began pacing the floor, fighting the fear that beat at him. If he had any kind of a chance, he would run. They could think what they wanted to. As Bonham had said, he could not prove his innocence here. He might, if he were free.

Free! The word hammered at his mind like the rhythmical roll of distant drums. Free! Free! Free! Only a free man had strength and will and the capacity to fight. Here he was like a wild horse in a corral. Now he understood how a stallion felt, driven in from the high open mesas to have his great heart broken; he knew why a stallion would fight until he killed himself or broke a leg and had to be killed.

Then, and he was not aware just how or why, the queer feeling of panic began to die. He thought of Peg who had gambled on him for protection just as she had gambled on the future, borrowing every cent she could from Brit Bonham. He thought of Shorty Avis who hated him because he hated and feared the Clawhammer, and of Rocky who had helped him.

Then, and he felt as if a sharp blade had been driven through him, he thought of Yuma Bill who had talked about planting good seeds. Kim had had a lifetime of freedom, but he had taken little of it to think. Now he had time. He sat quietly on his cot, his mind on Yuma Bill, and he realized that he had respected the little man for a very simple reason. Yuma Bill had lived the life he had talked. There could be no other reason for his coming here to help Brit Bonham. That was what he had meant when he had said that a man must find the things that lasted. He had found them, but Kim Logan never had.

It was close to evening when Ed Lane came with his meal—hot coffee, a thick steak, fried potatoes, and biscuits, the kind of meal Kim would have ordered if he had been in the hotel dining room.

"Thanks, Ed," he said.

"Thought you'd be getting a little lank," Lane said. "I told that China boy he'd better do a good job on that steak, or I'd have his pigtail."

Kim understood. Ed Lane knew what to expect tonight. He was not a man to die for an abstract principle called duty. As far as he was concerned, Kim Logan was a dead man swinging from a limb. By bringing this meal, Lane was easing his conscience. Later he would say he had done all he could.

When Kim finished, Lane took the plate, cup, and coffee pot.

"Time to put the feed bag on myself," he said, and left the jail.

X

Quiet came again after the last board had squeaked under Lane's feet, but it did not seem so oppressive. Kim emptied his sack of Durham and smoked the last cigarette. The sun was almost down now. He remembered the Dragon Peaks forming giant saw-teeth against the western sky, the vivid sweep of scarlet sunset, shadows darkening the edge of the valley and slowly moving across it. The world could be a good place to live, but seldom was that. There was a right and a wrong side to every human difference, but few sides were completely right or wrong. That was why there was so much trouble in the world, for it was natural that a man who had only a part of the right would think he had all of it.

Hank Dunning could probably make a case for himself. So, likely, had old Sam Cody. Even before that there were the gold seekers here, men too often without conscience. Perhaps it had always been that way. Kim only knew he had been a part of it, using his gun and dealing in death for those who could pay. He felt no pride in that. Nor could he change anything he had done. He rubbed out his cigarette, feeling none of the panic of the earlier afternoon. He realized that his were the thoughts of a man facing death.

When Lane returned with Bonham, the lawman again searched Bonham for a gun, then stepped back so that Bonham and Kim could talk.

"I found out a couple of things," Bonham said. "Dunning was in town until after you plugged Tonto Miles. Then he rode south. Mean anything?"

"Not much. How do you figure it?"

"Maybe Martin was holding Yuma prisoner out there till Dunning told him what to do. They wanted the *dinero* Yuma had on him, and they wanted you out of the way without having to dry-gulch you."

Kim nodded. "Could have been that way."

"I was the cause of it," the banker said bitterly. "If I hadn't . . ."

"None of that," Kim cut in. "I can say the same thing about myself. My mistake was in doing what Yuma wanted, but it sounded reasonable. A man just can't foresee things like this."

"It's pretty tough just the same," Bonham agreed.

"Smith?" Kim asked.

"I spent half the afternoon on the creek. He might have been fishing. The rain probably washed out any sign before I got there. I'm sure he ain't around now."

The last small hope was gone, but it was no more than Kim had expected.

"Peg?" he asked.

"She got my note," Bonham said heavily, "but I don't know what to expect. She just said thanks and went back into the house."

Kim gripped the bars, and felt again the emptiness that made him want to beat at the bars. He thought of men he had seen die with a rope on their necks. At the time there had seemed to be no doubt of their guilt. Rustling! Horse stealing! Killing! Now he wondered. Most of the men who would have a part in lynching him would have no doubt of his guilt. Johnny Naylor. Luke Haines. Vindictive Fred Galt. Men who had nothing to gain, small men who lacked the courage it took to stand against Hank Dunning.

"Kim." Bonham brought his mouth close to Kim's ear. "You're getting out of here right after dark. Be ready. One minute either way might decide it. Don't waste no time."

"I don't want you . . ."

"Don't make no difference whether you want it or not. I owe you the same kind of a debt that Yuma owed me. It's the rest of 'em I'm worried about. I'd do it myself, but I need help."

Bonham started across the room.

"Brit," Lane said.

Bonham made a slow turn to face him. Casually the sheriff opened a desk drawer and laid Kim's gun on the spur-scarred desk.

"I made a jackass out of myself this morning just like Logan said. So did Galt and Luke Haines and everybody else. We should have knowed the bank was good."

"You're a little late thinking of that," Bonham said.

"I am, for a fact." Lane laid a double-barreled shotgun on the desk beside Kim's Colt. "What I'm trying to say is that I know you're an honest man. You've done a lot for the country. Believed in it and stayed here. Even bucked old Sam Cody. Now you're an old man who deserves to die in bed with his boots off."

"I aim to," Bonham said evenly.

Lane gnawed off a chew of tobacco and slipped the plug back into his pocket.

"Naw, you don't aim to do no such thing. That whispering with Logan didn't fool nobody. You're fixing to bust him out of here. Now I'd hate to do it, but if you make a try, I'll drill you the same as I would any man."

Bonham threw his shoulders back. He said with dignity—"You'd be doing your duty, Ed."—and walked out.

The sheriff dropped into his swivel chair and cocked his legs on his desk. He said then: "I've been wondering, Logan. That *dinero* wasn't on you. What'd you do with it?"

"So that's it. I wondered what you was working up to."

Lane swung his feet to the floor. "I wasn't working up to nothing."

"But you'd make a deal, wouldn't you?"

"I don't savvy," Lane said, his face a mask of guile.

"If I split the *dinero* you think I stole, you'd shoot wide if Brit tries to break me out of here. That it?"

Lane choked. He spat into the brass spittoon at the end of his desk.

"I didn't make no such proposition."

"Yuma Bill had ten thousand dollars in his money belt, Ed. How would you like to have five of that?"

Lane sat down, scratching his baldhead. "I'm listening."

Kim wearily dropped down on his bunk.

"You don't need to think I'm goin' to get myself filled with lead to protect a killing son-of-a-bitch like you!" Lane bawled. "They'll haul you out of here tonight and you'll be dancing on air."

"I ain't surprised," Kim said. "No, sir. Dunning bought himself a sheriff when he pinned the star on you."

Lane leaned back in his chair. "I got the star, ain't I?" he said with smug satisfaction. "That's more'n you're getting from the Clawhammer. . . ."

Ed Lane had been in and out of his office all afternoon, apparently convinced that no effort would be made to break Kim out while it was daylight. With darkness upon the town, he stayed at his desk, feet cocked in front of him.

Kim watched the lamplight throwing a yellow glare on the man's shiny head. Kim wanted a cigarette, but his pride would not allow him to ask Lane for the makings.

He climbed up on the bunk and looked through the window. The sky was clear now; stars glittered with cold brilliance. The thunder had died away, but lightning still played along the horizon above the Continental Divide.

159

He sat down on his bunk again, impatience tightly winding his nerves. Usually a lynch mob gave out its own peculiar sound. Some of the men would be drunk. Others, probably Dunning and Fred Galt, would be cold sober. There would be no fight, Ed Lane being the man he was. Still, they must think of something that would make it appear that Lane had no responsibility for what was to happen.

Bonham would not be intimidated by what Lane had said. He and whoever was with him —Doc Frazee and Charlie Bemis—would make a try, but it was a question of which group would reach the jail first. If it came to a fight between them, Bonham was licked. Some of the mob would be HD hands, better fighting men than the few townsmen who would be siding Bonham.

A noise behind the courthouse startled Kim. Horse? He stepped up on the cot again. Three dark blobs out there might be horses, but he couldn't be sure. The starlight was so thin he might be seeing what he wanted to see and not what was actually out there.

Kim stepped down, saying casually: "Storm blew over."

"The big one ain't." Lane rose. "Too bad about Bonham. He's a fine old gent." He picked up the shotgun and sighted down the barrel. "Buckshot sure messes a man up. And don't count on

160

Bonham. One of Dunning's boys, Delaney, is outside. I ain't playing this alone."

Kim wanted to say that, if anything happened to Brit Bonham, Ed Lane would get his, too. But there was no use. Not unless Kim could get out of here with a gun in his hand. Whatever he said now would be an idle threat. He stood with his hands clenching the bars, hating Ed Lane as he had never hated a man before in his life.

The floor boards in the hall *squeaked*. Lane grinned and picked up the shotgun.

"Shut your eyes, Logan. This ain't goin' to be purty."

Quick steps sounded closer, then Kim's eyes widened as surprise shocked him. It was Della Naylor who came in. Lane was even more surprised than Kim. He stood staring at her uncertainly, then he laid the shotgun down and scratched his head.

"You gave me a turn, Della," Lane said. "I figured you was old man Bonham aiming to bust this killing son loose."

Della shook her head. "I'm not Bonham." She wrinkled her nose. "Or do I look like him?"

"Nope." Lane walked around the desk to her. "You're mighty purty, and you can't say that for that old goat."

She laughed. It struck Kim that there was a false note to it.

"Why ain't you home with Johnny?" he demanded.

She looked past Lane at Kim, frowning. "That's a smart question. I'll tell you. First place, Johnny isn't home. Second place, I've got an apology to make to Ed."

"Apology?" Lane reached out and patted her hands. "You don't need to make no apology to Ed Lane, not for nothing."

"Get out of here, Della!" Kim shouted,

"Well, you'd do well to keep your mouth shut," Della said. "Ed's the kind who appreciates a girl, which is more than I can say about Johnny. Or you, either."

Lane laughed easily. "That's sure true. Least-wise I appreciate you."

"Where's Rocky?" Kim demanded.

"Gone home." Della drew away from Lane and danced across the floor to Kim's cell, her back to Lane, hips swaying. "Johnny's in the Belle Union, getting drunk. Both cats are away, Ed. No reason the mouse shouldn't play."

"I wouldn't mind playing mouse," Lane said.

Della danced back toward the door. "About that apology, Ed. If I'd known Kim had killed that poor old man, I'd never have made Johnny back up on his story. Rocky likes Kim. I just did it because she asked me to."

"Rocky's mistook, too," Lane said. "He's not worth much, Logan ain't."

Della stood in the doorway, scowling at Kim. Then she shrugged.

"Well," she said, "he'll get what he's got coming to him. Rocky's the only one who'll be sorry." She started to turn, saying to the sheriff over her shoulder: "You going to be here all night, Ed?"

"I don't figure on it."

Lane took a step toward her, but she moved back into the dark hall, as elusive as a shadow.

"Now, Ed," she said. "What are you up to?"

"What are you up to coming here?" he demanded.

"To tell you I made a mistake about Kim." She laughed lightly. "And that Johnny isn't home, but that doesn't mean anything to you."

"How do I know you ain't hoorawing me?"

This time Della stood motionlessly while Lane came up to her. He put his arms around her, the lamplight falling past them, their single shadow darkening the middle of the yellow patch. Della offered her lips.

"I wouldn't fool you, Ed," she whispered.

Lane kissed her avidly, his attention so fixed that he was not aware of it when Rocky slipped out of a dark corner behind him. She hit him with the barrel of her gun, an upsweeping blow that brought him to his knees. He was too tall for her to have done more. He tried to call out, but only a groaning, muffled sound came out of him. Rocky jammed a wadded-up bandanna into his mouth and swung the gun again. He went limp and she stepped away and let him fall.

"Good job," Della said, running into Lane's office. "How do you like my acting, Kim?"

"Too good. I wish you hadn't got into this."

Della grabbed Lane's keys from his desk and tried one in the lock of Kim's cell. It failed. A second failed, but the third turned the lock, and Della pulled the door open. Rocky had come in and stood watching, trembling under the nervous pressure of the moment.

"Let's lock him up," Della said. "It won't help Ed's reputation any if they find him locked up in your cell."

Kim dragged Lane's limp body into the cell and locked the door, wondering how badly he was hurt. Blood trickled in a small scarlet stream across the lawman's baldhead. Kim scooped up his gun, and slid it into holster.

"Horses are in back," Rocky said. "Here!" She pressed a sack of Durham and a package of cigarette papers into his hand.

Kim said—"Thanks."—and blew out the lamp, bringing total blackness.

Della was halfway down the hall. Rocky gripped Kim's arm.

"The front door is propped open," she said, "but we can't just make a run for it. Pete Delaney's outside. He knows we're in here, so we've got to take care of him."

"Can't shoot him," Kim said. "Bring the whole wolf pack."

"Maybe we can work it like we did on Lane. You stay in the hall. Della's going to fetch Delaney in if she can."

They moved toward the front door. Apparently Della had reached the steps. "Pete!" she called.

A man drifted up out of the darkness. "Anything wrong?"

"Plenty," came Della's worried voice. "Come here and look."

Rocky and Kim were at the end of the hall, where the faint light from the street was falling through the open doorway. Kim moved close to the wall and remained inside the hall, but Rocky went on outside, to stand beside Della.

"Hurry, Pete," Rocky said with quiet urgency. "The light's out, and we can't find our way."

The HD man swore. "You don't reckon Bonham got Logan out, do you?" he asked.

"It's as black as a tomb in there," Rocky breathed. "We couldn't see. Maybe somebody shot Kim!"

"No such luck as that," Delaney growled, and started up the steps. He reached the top one and stopped, suddenly suspicious. "What kind of a trick are you two trying on me? Ed had a light back there a minute ago."

"He hasn't now," Rocky said. "Have you got any matches?"

Rocky and Della were both on the top step, with Delaney between them. For a moment he stood motionlessly, turning his head to look at one and then the other of the girls.

"Yeah, I've got a match," he said finally, "but I ain't going in there. Maybe you're sweet on Logan, Rocky. Maybe you got him out of his cell, and, when I go in there, he'll burn me down."

"I just want to see him get a square deal!" Rocky flared. "I want to know what happened."

"I guess you're afraid of the dark," Della said scornfully. "Give me a match and I'll find out what's wrong."

"I ain't afraid of the dark," Delaney said, "but I'm afraid of Kim Logan, and I ain't the only one. I'm goin' to get Dunning."

Delaney swung around to go back down the steps, but before he'd made the full turn, the girls grabbed his arms.

"Kim!" Rocky called.

Delaney bawled a surprised oath, and jerked his hands free, slamming both girls back against the courthouse wall, but it was something he had not expected, and it took a moment. Before he could lift his gun, Kim was on him.

Kim got his left arm around Delaney's neck and squeezed, while he drove his right into the HD man's face. Delaney gurgled and tried to break free, but his frantic threshing accomplished nothing. His back was against Kim's stomach, and the best he could do was to lash backward with a foot, catching Kim on the shin.

"Bust him!" Della urged. "Somebody's coming!"

XI

Given time, Kim could have choked the HD man unconscious, but there was no time. Once the alarm was sounded, a dozen men would rush out of the Belle Union and Rocky and Della might get hurt. This was what Brit Bonham had foreseen might happen when he had warned Kim to be ready.

Kim pulled Delaney back into the hall, then he let go. Delaney went down, half-stunned, his head rapping against the floor. Kim dropped on him, driving breath out of him. He swung his right fist to Delaney's jaw. When he arose, Delaney lay still.

Kim plunged through the doorway. Rocky and Della were already at the foot of the steps.

"This way, Kim," Rocky said softly.

He glimpsed their shadowy figures fading toward the corner of the building. A man turning in from the street heard their running footsteps.

"Dunning!" he yelled, and fired, a wild, high shot. Kim ran after the girls, hit a wet spot, and fell headlong. He scrambled up as the man threw another shot that went wide, and sprinted on, reaching the rear of the courthouse as Della swung into saddle.

"I'm going home, Kim!" Della called. "Don't get into a fight with 'em. I don't want Johnny hurt." She rode away.

"Here." Bonham pressed a horse's reins into Kim's hands. "Do what Rocky says. She's got it all planned."

Rocky was in the saddle now, calling in a hurry-up tone: "Come on, come on!"

Kim mounted. "What'd you get the girls into this for, Brit?" he demanded.

"Rocky's idea, not mine," Bonham said, and drifted away into the darkness.

Rocky was already riding into the cluster of deserted cabins back of the courthouse, her horse's hoofs dropping into the soft earth with faint sounds. The hoof beats of Della's running horse came clearly, heading toward the mesa.

Kim reined in beside Rocky.

"I can't let her go alone," he said angrily. "They're likely to kill her before they find out who she is."

"Don't be a fool," Rocky said sharply. "She's got the fastest horse in the valley and she's the best rider. They'll never catch her. Or if they do, all she'll have to do is holler. Johnny'll be with the posse."

Rocky turned into an old shed and dismounted. For a moment Kim sat his saddle, fighting his stubborn pride. Then he stepped down beside Rocky, knowing she was right. If he followed Della, there would be a fight, and in the posse would be men Kim did not want to kill.

A great *clatter* had broken out in front of the courthouse. Men shouted; there was some wild shooting. Then Dunning's great voice: "We're losing time! I'll take charge here!" A moment later eight or ten riders swept out of town, but already the hoof beats of Della's mount had faded. In this vast blanket of darkness there would be little chance of finding her.

Kim gripped Rocky's arm and turned her to face him.

"Why did you and Della do this?" he asked.

"We've got a fight on our hands," she said. "When you finally get Peg figured out, you'll lead us. We couldn't let them hang a man we needed."

"I don't think Dutch Heinz meant . . ."

"Oh, yes, he did. We're not going to run again. Maybe you don't know it, but Dad and Della's father and most of our neighbors were driven out of the valley by Sam Cody. We won't be driven again, Kim. Not by Peg or Dunning or anybody!"

He had never asked who had suffered from Sam Cody's pushing tactics because he had not considered it his business. Naturally Peg had not volunteered much information about it. Now he understood Shorty Avis's hatred for everything that belonged to the Clawhammer. Rocky's father had classed him with Heinz.

"We'd better ride," Kim said.

For a moment Rocky did not move. Her face was still lifted to his as if her eyes were trying to pierce the darkness.

"I was pretty young," she said, "so I don't remember much about the trouble, but I've heard Dad say that if they had fought together, they could have licked Cody. It'll be the same again unless somebody can make us work together."

It was the old, time-proven technique of divide and conquer. A single large outfit could clear a range of small spreads by taking them one at a time, but if they had united, the small spreads would have been stronger than their common enemy. To weld a bunch of small cowmen together was always a problem. Kim, knowing the mesa ranchers, doubted that it could be done.

"I'm beholden to you," Kim said at last, "and, if it comes to a fight, I'm your man. I don't think it will. Peg's got all she can do to hold Dunning off, without bothering you folks."

Rocky stepped into the saddle. She waited until Kim had swung up. Then she said: "It would be an accident if we ran into them tonight. By sunup we'll be hid out."

"I'm not going to dodge around like a rabbit," Kim said hotly.

"Then go back and sit in jail. If you want your neck stretched, they'll accommodate you."

They threaded their way through the cabins until they reached open country, then swung toward the stage road that crossed the valley. Reaching it, they turned directly east until they came to the side road that led to the Clawhammer. Kim reined up.

"You go on home and stay out of trouble," he said.

"Where are you going?"

"To the Clawhammer."

"You don't think you'll get the man who killed Yuma Bill out there, do you?"

"I might."

"Or maybe you think Peg will hide you."

"I've got to have grub. Only thing to do is to duck the posse till I get my hands on Phil Martin. When I do, he'll sing another tune."

She took a ragged breath, her saddle *squeaking* as she shifted her weight. "Kim, you think we hate the Clawhammer so much that we're judging Peg wrong. That it?"

"That's about it. Peg's into trouble up to her neck. Looks like your bunch and the Clawhammer had better throw in together, or Dunning will have the valley."

"I've never told you what I know about Peg," she said reluctantly, "because you wouldn't believe me. You'd just say I hated her. I do, but hating her doesn't make me blind. You are."

"I don't go switching around when I take a job," he said hotly. "Sure Peg's greedy, but that ain't a crime."

"I'll ride along with you," she said. "If you find out she doesn't want anything to do with you now, will you go with me?"

"Sure. But what'll you do if you're guessing wrong on Peg?"

"I'm not," she said.

Rocky turned off the stage road, following the twin ruts that led to Clawhammer. Kim caught up with her, admitting to himself that she might be right about his being blind. It had always been a fault with him, believing in people he wanted to believe in until the evidence was final. Loyalty could be a fault as well as a virtue. Peg's faith in Dutch Heinz proved that.

A shadow as dark as this night lay upon the valley, evil that had brought about the death of Yuma Bill and had nearly put a rope around Kim's neck. The trouble was that both evil and good were often disguised as the other. Now, with the cool night wind on his face and the tension of the long afternoon finally lifted, he had time to think about Yuma Bill's death. Dutch Heinz could have been the killer. Peg could have told him that Yuma would be at Smith's cabin. That brought him squarely back to Peg. It was what Rocky would have him believe, but he could not.

It was near midnight when Kim and Rocky forded Ganado Creek, water lancing out from their horses' hoofs like curving arrows, faintly silvered by the starlight. The big ranch house sprawled before them. The place seemed quiet; there was no light anywhere.

"You can't stay here long, Kim," Rocky said. "When they don't pick up your trail, they'll come here."

"I reckon," Kim agreed.

The dog charged around the corner of the house, barking fiercely. Kim reined up, calling: "Shut up, Nero!" He swung down, looping his reins over the hitch pole. The dog jumped around, whining eagerly, and Kim stooped to pet him.

Kim expected a light to come to life inside the house, but there was none. Then old Limpy called out from the darkness:

"Who is it?"

"Kim."

"Who's with you?"

"Rocky Avis."

There was a moment of silence. Limpy, Kim was sure, would doubt the girl's presence. Then the old man drifted up, thumbing a match to flame. The tiny light briefly showed the girl's face, her dark eyes filled with cool defiance. Then the match flickered out.

"Didn't believe it, did you, Limpy?" Rocky asked.

"No, I sure didn't," the old man admitted. "What you doing here, Rocky?"

"Company for Kim."

"Maybe I'd better ask what you're doing here, Kim? Thought you was in the calaboose for beefing that *hombre* you took off the stage."

"Kicked a couple bars loose. Sure didn't get no help from the Clawhammer."

"Didn't have no help to give you," Limpy snapped. "If you had some powder to burn, why didn't you burn it on one of Dunning's toughs?"

"You making out I drilled Yuma?"

"Lane had an eyewitness, the way we heard it."

"Phil Martin," Kim said hotly. "You believe him?"

"Maybe," the old man said. "Maybe not. All I know is we don't want a hunted man hiding out on the Clawhammer."

"You see?" Rocky said quietly. "He's been told what to say."

Kim wheeled and started toward the house.

"Come back here!" Limpy called. "Peg's been asleep for a couple of hours."

"She'll wake up," Kim said, and went on.

"You come back here!" Limpy bawled. "I've got a Winchester. . . ."

"But you won't use it," Rocky said. "I've got a gun, too."

Limpy subsided, muttering. Kim went into the house and lit a lamp. Then he crossed to Peg's

174

door and tapped. There was no response. He tapped again, louder. Another moment of silence, then Peg called sleepily: "Who is it?"

"Kim. I've got to talk to you."

"Wait till I get my robe on."

He moved back to the table and stood there, worriedly tapping his fingers on the oak surface. He wondered what he would say. He wouldn't tell her he was riding out of the valley to duck a killing charge. Besides, she still needed him.

He heard her door open, and looked up. She was wearing a dark blue robe, her hair falling down her back in a red mass. She came to him with quick eagerness, her hands out. She put her arms around him, and she clung to him for a moment. Then she tipped her head back, eyes anxiously searching his face.

"I've been worried about you, Kim. Bonham sent word you were in jail. How did you get out?"

Rocky was wrong about her. That was Kim's first thought. Perhaps he was blind to Peg Cody's faults, but regardless of those faults, she had been anxious about him.

"I'm out," he said. "That's what counts. I've been doing some worrying myself. You still haven't got anybody here but Limpy. Nothing to keep Dunning from wiping you out."

"He won't," she said with some impatience. "I keep telling you that. You're the one who's in trouble."

"I won't be soon as I get the truth out of Martin. He's the one who tried to put the rope around my neck. Another one of Dunning's tricks, I reckon."

She shook her head. "You won't be any help to the Clawhammer if they get that rope on your neck, Kim. You've got to get out of the valley and stay out."

He frowned, searching her face. He could not keep doubt from nagging at his mind.

"I'm not getting out yet," he said roughly. "I've got to buy some time, Peg. That's all I need."

"I can't help you, Kim." She shook her head. "I shouldn't have said that, I suppose, but I know you wouldn't want to pull me into trouble with the law."

When he had come here, he had had no intention of staying. What he had wanted was to prove Rocky wrong. Now he said: "You could hide me out."

"I'd like to help you, Kim, but the best thing for both of us is for you to put a lot of miles between you and Ganado."

He was trying to see something in her face that wasn't there. Her eyes seemed to hold concern for him, but he could not tell what was behind them. Women, he thought, were natural born actresses. Della Naylor had fooled Ed Lane, and he himself had a hunch that Peg was fooling him now as effectively as Della had fooled Lane.

He took a deep breath, remembering the

dreams he had never confided to anyone. The Clawhammer might have been all he had hoped for, his and Peg's, if he could have proved to her she needed him. Not in the way she needed Dutch Heinz, but in the way a woman needs one particular man, prove it so that she would obey the desires of her heart instead of the logic of her mind.

He thought of Tonto Miles, remembered facing him in the morning sunlight. They were the same, two men hired for their guns, yet there had been the hope that he was more than that to Peg Cody. Now he sensed that he had made the mistake of reaching for something he could never possess. He had found only the shadow, not the substance.

"You want me to run?" he demanded. "Let folks think I killed Yuma?"

"You've got to," she said. "Don't you see? The Clawhammer can't protect a man who's wanted by the law."

"Looks like it ought to make some difference who the man is."

She shook her head. "Not when it concerns the Clawhammer."

He made one quick step and took her into his arms. He kissed her, trying to put everything into that kiss that he could not put into words. He failed. He realized it at once. There had been something in her last night—a demand, a hunger for him. It was not in her now.

He let her go and stepped back to the table. "I didn't ask you to marry me last night because I wanted you to feel that I could do something for you. I mean, something bigger than just riding and making a show of my gun and seeing that Dunning stayed on his side of the creek. I did it today. It was something you couldn't have bought for all the dollars in the valley."

"I know," she said coolly. "You saved the bank and Dunning didn't get my notes. But Lane arrested you for a killing. That changes everything."

"For a killing I didn't do!" he said hotly. "That shouldn't change anything. You're the one who's changing things."

She shook her head. "I threw myself at you and you threw me back. You changed both our lives for us then." She made a quick gesture as if dismissing it forever. "It's a poor kind of woman who has no pride. I have mine, Kim."

"You threw the Clawhammer at me, not yourself. Maybe someday you'll find you're a woman, not a ranch." He turned toward the door, but swung back before he reached it. "Yuma Bill didn't sleep any last night. He said he heard you ride out before dawn."

Her lips made a tight line; wariness crept into her eyes.

"He dreamed it," she said coldly.

"I don't think so." He was grim now. "I'm pretty

good at forgetting things I don't want to remember, but there's one thing I can't forget. It was you who had the idea for Yuma to stay at Smith's cabin while I rode into town. He was killed at the cabin."

"Go on," she breathed. "Say the rest of it."

"I don't need to say it. Heinz wanted to kill Yuma last night for the *dinero* that was in the shoe box."

"And I said no. Remember?"

"Yeah, I remember. But after that you had time to think it over."

"Go on, Kim," she challenged. "Say it. Say that I killed Yuma Bill!"

XII

Kim stood looking at Peg Cody, nagged by a suspicion that had been in his mind all through the afternoon. Still, even after all of this, he could not put it in words.

"I'll be riding," he said, and turned again toward the door.

"Kim." She gripped his arm and turned him to face her. "You know now that the only thing I really love is the Clawhammer."

He nodded. "I guess that's plain enough. You're making a mistake, Peg. You'll come out holding the short end of the stick."

"I'll take my chances."

From outside Rocky called: "Kim, they're coming!"

"Who's that?" Peg asked, startled.

"Rocky Avis."

"You mean . . . ?" Peg began to laugh. "Well, I've been a bigger fool than I ever thought I'd be. You've been in love with Shorty Avis's brat all the time. I asked you last night and you lied to me."

Her anger swiftly swelled to a wild fury. She would believe what she wanted to believe.

"Reckon I'm fired," he said.

"You bet you're fired! If you're smart, you'll keep riding till you're a thousand miles from here, and don't think you can stay and save your friends on the mesa. The Clawhammer needs all the range on this side of the creek. All of it! Do you hear?" Her voice rose until it was the scream of a shrew. "I'm building an empire, but I don't need your help. Keep riding, and take the Avis kid with you!"

This was the first time she had ever whipped him with her tongue. Her eyes were bright with fury, her face was red, and her mouth working. Then it occurred to him that she wanted to feel she owed him nothing.

Rocky called again, more urgently: "Kim, they're coming!"

"So long, Peg," he said, and left the house.

"You'd better travel, mister," Limpy said. "I'll steer 'em the wrong way. The Clawhammer owes you that much."

"Thanks, Limpy." Kim mounted. "So long."

"This way!" Rocky called.

The posse was coming in on the road that Kim and Rocky had followed minutes before. Rocky turned south. Kim swung in beside her, surprised, for he had supposed she would want to go home. To do that, she would have to cross the creek and swing west. Instead, she followed the bench to the left, an indistinct wall in the darkness.

They rode slowly, their horses' hoofs making little sounds in the soft grass carpet. The racket made by the posse died, then Dunning called out: "We're looking for Kim Logan! Seen him?"

Kim could not hear what Limpy said. He wondered what Peg would say. When he had left her, she had been furious enough to want to see him lynched. He doubted whether her anger had cooled so that she would cover up for him.

Kim expected pursuit, but there was none. Either Peg had lied for him, or Limpy had sent the posse across the creek on a wild-goose chase.

The lights in the ranch house became tiny pinpoints, then were lost to sight. Presently Rocky said: "There's a trail here. We'll swing up on the mesa."

They were perhaps three miles south of the creek.

"I don't savvy this," Kim said. "You're putting the cañon between us and your place."

"That's exactly what I aim to do. We're not going to my place. Limpy will tell them who was with you, so they'll hightail up there."

Kim laughed. "Shorty'll sure be surprised."

"He'll be mighty mad," she said worriedly. "He won't like you sashaying around through the hills with me."

"I know he won't. If I ever go home, he'll rawhide me, and maybe get out his shotgun and make you marry me."

"He wouldn't need his shotgun for that."

She didn't say anything then. They climbed to the sage flat above the bench to open country, dotted by runty cedars. A slim moon was showing above the peaks; the stars still glittered in cold brilliance from a clear, wind-swept sky.

Rocky reined up and, untying her coat from behind her saddle, slipped into it.

"You know, Kim," she said, her voice expressionless, "I wouldn't care for a marriage that needed a shotgun."

"It wouldn't . . ."

"No, don't say that. You've had Peg in your mind for a long time. I don't know whether you ever really loved her or not. Maybe you were in love with the Clawhammer. Either way, it'll take some time to get it out of your system."

He rolled a smoke and lighted it, the flame

throwing a brief light upon his wide mouth and square chin. "You got some pretty sorry notions about me, Rocky," he said. "I can't figure out why you've gone to so much trouble for me lately."

"Not sorry notions, Kim. It's just that you're two men."

"Never knew I was twins," he jeered.

"I've known it for a long time. There's the man you have been and the man you could be. I keep wondering which one you're finally going to be."

"Makes me quite a mess, don't it?"

"It'll be a mess if you ride out of the country now," she said. "Someday men like you will disappear, but that day hasn't come yet. Maybe it's a good thing. We need you."

"You think the country will be better off if men like me disappear?"

"Yes. I mean, the man you have been. Anyhow, I couldn't blame you if you did ride on."

"I couldn't," he said quietly. "There's plenty here to hold me."

"You mean you wouldn't leave a killer charge?"

"That's part of it."

"What's the rest?"

"You ain't ready to hear about it."

"I'm ready to listen when you're ready to tell it."

"Maybe I won't have to tell it."

They went on, the flat gradually lifting toward the rim in front of them. Presently they were in the timber, limbs interlacing above them and blotting out the starlight. Rocky rode ahead, following the twisting narrow trail in a way that brought increasing admiration for her in Kim's mind.

They stopped at a spring to water their horses when the first gray hint of dawn was touching the eastern sky.

"Almost there," Rocky said.

"You're riding through this country like you knew it," Kim remarked.

"I do. I like to ride at night. Pa claims I'm half owl."

They took the trail again, climbing steep pitches, crossing small parks and coming into the timber again, their horses' hoofs dropping silently into the thick mat of pine needles that was seldom disturbed except by the swift passage of a deer. They splashed across a small stream and Rocky swung to follow it.

Daylight had moved in, but the air was still sharp with the last of the night chill.

Another five minutes brought them to a cabin at the end of a long stretch of aspens that made a splash of light green against the darker pines.

"This is it," Rocky said, and swung down.

She stood there for a moment, one hand holding to the saddle horn, bone weary.

"We should have stopped," Kim said. "You're all in."

"Not quite." She gave him a quick smile that

was a light on her face. "They'll never find us here. We can sleep for a week."

"Us? Look here, Rocky, I'm not going to let 'em find you with me!"

"You'll have a hard time getting rid of me." She motioned to a shed behind the cabin. "Put the horses up. I'll get breakfast."

She had not brought any food. He wondered what she would find for breakfast, but when he finished with the horses and went in, aspen chunks were burning in the stove with bright crackling pops, and the cabin was filled with the fragrance of boiling coffee and frying bacon.

"How did you . . . ?"

She turned from the stove, brushing at a stray strand of hair that fell across her forehead. "Magic. I said hocus pocus. Then I waved my hands and said abracadabra."

"I didn't know you were that smart."

He looked around, his amazement growing. The timber around Pass Creek Valley was full of prospectors' cabins, but none that Kim had seen were like this. It was clean and tight, with a bunk at one end, the stove at the other, and a small pine table and two benches in the middle. Shelves behind the stove were filled with cans of food.

Rocky motioned to a bucket on the packed dirt floor.

"Fetch in some more water, will you, Kim?"

When he returned, she had poured the coffee.

"This isn't much of a breakfast," she said, "but it'll do." She yawned. "I'm about to fall over in my tracks. I didn't get much sleep the night before, either. By the time I took the body in . . ."

"Body? You mean you took that *hombre* in who fell off the cliff?"

She laughed shakily. "I wasn't going to tell you that. I just didn't have time to go home and get Pa. Besides, I wanted to be in town when you and Yuma Bill got there." She dropped down on one of the benches, suddenly defiant. "I wasn't sure Pa would do it. He's awful stubborn sometimes."

He stood looking down at her, more humble than he had ever been before in his life. He had always thought of her as more girl than woman, probably because she was small, or perhaps because she seemed child-like. Now he realized that what he had considered childishness was not that at all. She was a product of the life she lived—simple, without pretense or sham, honest with herself and others, and with a courage that few men could claim.

"If I live a million years," he said, "I'll never be able to pay you."

"Sit down," she broke in sharply. "You don't owe me anything. The trouble with you is that you've always thought there was nothing you and your gun couldn't do. You're going to find out different."

"I have already," he said, and took the bench across the table from her.

It was late afternoon when Kim awoke. He had gone to sleep in the shadow of the shed. Now the sun had moved far to the west and was drenching him with its warmth. He got up and, walking to the creek, washed his face. He had a brief glimpse of himself in the unruffled surface of a deep pool and shook his head in disapproval. He needed a shave, his yellow hair was matted and overlong, and his face seemed gaunter than ever.

"You look pretty tough, fella," he said aloud.

He hunkered beside the stream in the shade of a pine and rolled a smoke. Constant riding had honed his long body down to skin and hard muscle and bone; never-ending vigilance had cut lines around his eyes that made him look years older than he was. Now, and it seemed as if it were the first time in months, he felt no need for vigilance. He was at peace. The impending violence that had long threatened the valley would still be like a stream running in full flood, but at this moment it seemed remote.

A jay flew by, a flash of vivid blue. Overhead a woodpecker was working on a tree with jackhammer violence. Below him a foot-long trout flashed across the pool like a black, knifing shadow. Kim had been too busy trying to keep alive in a world of trouble to notice things like this. This was another world, Rocky's world. She shared its strength and honesty; it had made her what she was.

It was strange, he thought, how he had lived in country like this most of his life, yet actually he had not known it at all. He had merely passed through it. He flipped his cigarette stub into the creek and lay back, staring at the clean sky.

There was no wind, just the quiet steady downpouring of the sun's rays. Here were the smells of a moist earth and pine needles and wildflowers, all flowing together into one common mountain smell. Here were sounds—the *squawking* of the jay, the rhythmical *clattering* of the woodpecker, the creek song as it dropped over a rock ledge above the pool, sounds that fell together as naturally as those from a trained orchestra and, paradoxically, did not mar the great silence.

He did not know that Rocky had come up behind him until she asked: "Sleeping?"

Kim jumped and rolled and grabbed for his gun, the natural reaction of a man who has long lived with danger as a daily companion. Then he lay motionlessly, staring up at her and feeling foolish. He started to tell her never to sneak up on him like that again, but he caught himself in time. She hadn't sneaked up on him. It was her natural way of moving.

"No," he said. "Dreaming, I guess. How'd you sleep?"

"I didn't. I just died."

He sat up, feeling of his stubbly chin. "I took a look at myself a while ago. Sure handsome."

"You look natural." She dropped down beside him. "I didn't tell you this morning, but I think Brit will be along, so I might as well. This is his cabin."

He reached for the makings. "Comes out to fish, I suppose."

"No. He thinks this is still mining country. He's got a prospect hole across the creek." She motioned. "Over behind that brush. He tells folks in town that he comes up here to fish, but it's really to dig."

"How did you know about his cabin?"

"I stumbled onto it during a storm. Brit was here. He made me promise I'd make all my children be hard-rock miners if I ever told anybody, but that won't apply to you. He knew I was bringing you here."

"Sure would be awful, having your children turn out to be hard-rock miners."

She laughed. "It would for a fact. I like it on top of the ground."

"So that's why there was grub."

She nodded. "He keeps enough here to last two or three weeks. He was snowed in once."

"Funny a banker would get the notion he was a prospector."

"Not so funny. Doc Frazee's the same. They'd

189

like to see Ganado come back and the only way they know to bring it back is to have another mining boom." She lay on the bank, her slim body curled so that the hem of her riding skirt had worked up to her knees. She didn't notice; her eyes were on the pool, her tanned face eagerly alert. "Kim, there's enough trout down there for supper! Want me to get Brit's pole for you?"

"I wouldn't know what to do with a fish if he reached up and hollered for me to pull him out," he said ruefully.

She rolled over, tugging at her skirt. "You mean you've never gone fishing?"

"Not since I was a kid. Been too busy."

For no reason that Kim could see, she was suddenly angry. "Too busy! If all you've done was to ride around stomping snakes, you'd better start fishing!"

He had smoked his cigarette down and thrown the stub into the creek. Automatically he reached for paper and tobacco and rolled another, sensing the same scorn that had been in her when he had stopped with Yuma Bill and she had talked about him being a snake stomper. He said nothing until he lighted his cigarette. She was sitting up, chin resting on her knees, dark eyes staring morosely at the big pine across the creek.

"Ever figure you might have me wrong?" he asked.

"No. I don't, either. There's a place for fighting and a place for work, but you don't know anything about the work. Just fighting."

He grinned, the cigarette dangling from one corner of his mouth, the blue smoke curling up lazily before his lean face. "Maybe I'm a better snake stomper than a brush popper, but I've done a little staring at the rear end of a cow, too. I helped drive a Texas herd plumb to Dakota. Surprised?"

"I sure am," she said skeptically. "I didn't think you'd ever take a chance on ruining your gun hand with a rope or a branding iron."

"Here's another surprise. I've got a thousand dollars in Bonham's bank. Saved it since I got here. Had a notion I'd like to own a little outfit. Up by your place, maybe. Anyhow, I thought I'd keep on working for Peg as long as I could, so I'd have a stake when I started."

"You might try poker," she jeered.

"Naw, I'm about as bad as Johnny Naylor. That's why I was broke when I got here." He tossed a rock into the creek and watched the ripples spread across the pool. "Just before I left Yuma Bill yesterday morning, he said something about throwing in with me and buying a ranch here in the valley."

She stared at him for a long moment, lips parted as she thought about what he had said. "When he was killed, you lost your chance."

"Any chance except what I make myself." He nodded. "A man don't buy many cows and calves with a thousand dollars."

"Well, I am surprised," Rocky said. "It's the other side of you I was talking about."

He grinned wryly. "I've done some thinking, but not much talking. I did a lot more thinking after I met Yuma Bill. Seems like I can't forget the *hombre* who fell off the rim. And Tonto Miles. Sooner or later I'll get the same." He threw his cigarette away in a sudden violent gesture. "A man can't help dying alone, but it's the devil and all to live alone."

"I know," she breathed. She stiffened and was silent, head cocked. "Somebody's coming up the trail. Must be Brit. I'll get supper. You cut some wood."

XIII

Rocky jumped up and ran into the cabin. Kim sat listening, but he heard nothing. He got up, shaking his head. Compared to most of the men he had ridden with, his ears were good, but Rocky made him feel like a greenhorn.

There was a pile of dry aspen in one corner of the shed; an axe leaned against the wall. He began to chop, watching the trail below the cabin, and presently Brit Bonham appeared. Kim carried an armload of wood into the cabin, and, when he came out, Bonham had dismounted.

"Well, I see you outran 'em," Bonham said. "Figured you would. Don't reckon nobody in the country knows these hills like Rocky does, unless it's Della."

Kim told him what had happened. "Dunning get back to town?" he asked.

Bonham shook his head. "Hadn't when I left. Kind of worries me. Dunning sure don't like failures, and so far that's all he's had. Can't do no damage, though, I guess."

"He can go after the Clawhammer."

Bonham's brows lifted. "Thought you said Peg fired you."

"She did, but I still don't cotton to the notion of Dunning moving across the creek."

"Well, Peg's old Sam Cody's daughter, and I reckon he taught her how to take care of herself. . . . Catch any fish?"

"No."

"Then take care of my mare. I'll catch our supper."

By the time Kim had finished staking out the mare and cut another armload of wood, Bonham had pulled three pan-size trout out of the pool. He cleaned and brought them in.

"Can't understand a man not fishing when he's got a chance. Good for your soul, Kim."

Rocky looked up from setting the table. "He's never had time to learn, Brit."

Bonham snorted. "Say, when a man hasn't got time to fish, he's almighty busy. Want me to fry 'em, Rocky?"

"Go ahead," she said.

It was a silent meal, with Kim feeling a sudden impatience at this inactivity. Finishing his coffee, he arose and walked to the door. The sun was down now, and the timber had blotted up most of the thinning light. Rocky had lighted a lamp, and Kim's shadow made a long dark splotch in the rectangle of lamplight, spilling out through the doorway.

He rolled a smoke, thinking. He couldn't stay here, and he couldn't go back to Ganado. Still, if Phil Martin was in town, that was where Kim must go. Martin had placed the killer charge against him, so Martin was the one who could clear him.

Without turning, Kim asked: "Martin still in Ganado?"

"Yeah. Doc's keeping him. Seems like he should have gone to bed instead of sashaying around. Now he's a purty sick man."

"Brit, did you know that Yuma Bill was going into the cattle business here?" Rocky asked. "He was planning on taking Kim in as a partner."

"Well, I ain't surprised," Bonham said. "He sold out most of his holdings around Las Animas. I figured he'd stay hereabouts, and he couldn't have kept his fingers off a ranch."

"What's going to happen to the money Kim brought to you?" Rocky asked.

"Well, that's something I've been asking myself," Bonham said somberly. "I doubt that Yuma left a will, and I know he didn't have a single living relative."

"Then he'd want you to have it, you and Kim, wouldn't he?"

"I guess he would."

"Then why don't you buy a big herd and let Kim have his ranch?"

Kim walked back to the table. "She's trying to make a working man out of me."

"It's what you want, isn't it?" Rocky demanded.

"I told you it was, but taking a dead man's money don't seem the right way to get it."

"Maybe marrying a redhead with a ranch would be?" Rocky flared.

"Maybe."

"It'd be right enough, Kim," Bonham said slowly. "As soon as I see the bank ain't goin' to need it, I wouldn't be against doing something like that, only . . ." He paused, looking from Rocky to Kim, his face thoughtful.

"Only what?" Rocky asked.

Bonham got up and stood with his back to the stove, his craggy face mirroring uncertainty. "I just ain't sure. You see, Rocky, me and Doc Frazee and Charlie Bemis, well, we're old. Younger men now, they ain't what you'd call real solid."

"Say the rest of it, Brit," Kim said tonelessly. "I'm a fiddle-foot who's likely to be dragging out of here tomorrow."

"Well, cuss it, you are," Bonham said, "and there ain't nobody else who can put the brake on Dunning. Or Peg, neither, if she gets some of old Sam's ideas."

"She's already got them. Brit, you're forgetting one thing." Rocky leaned forward. "My people."

Bonham gestured impatiently. "And you're forgetting that when Sam Cody made a few faces at 'em, they tucked their tails and lined out for the mesa. Old Sam moved in. The east side of the valley is Clawhammer range whether you like it or not. Now that money is a kind of trust, you might say, and I've got to decide what to do with it along the line of what Yuma Bill would want."

"Like planting the right seed?" Kim said.

Bonham gave him a defiant glance. "I don't know if you're trying to hooraw me or not, but that's exactly what I mean. He kind of stole that money in the first place. Then he got a change of heart, but there wasn't no way to give it back, so he was bent on doing some good with it."

"Wouldn't it be good to bring peace to the valley?" Rocky asked.

Bonham shook his head. "I ain't sure that putting Kim on a ranch would stop Dunning or

Peg, Rocky. The big fight's still ahead, and I doubt we've got enough on our side to win it."

"I'm going back to Ganado," Kim said, "and I'll get a different story out of Martin."

"Doc Frazee's working on Martin already." Bonham came back to the table. "Kim, where would you have gone if you'd been Salty Smith?"

"Wouldn't be north. No place to go. Wouldn't be west, 'cause that'd take him past Dunning's spread. He'd have a rough trip getting into New Mexico if he went south. So I reckon he'd head for the pass and go to Del Norte."

Bonham laughed. "That's the way everybody but Smith would figure. Not old Salty, though. He'd ask himself what folks would expect him to do, then he'd cross 'em up. He headed south, but he didn't try getting across the line. He's in Sky City."

"He couldn't hide in a pueblo like that. Dunning's sure to find him."

"That's what I figure. If he does, he'll shut Smith's mouth for good, but Smith thinks he's safe. Fatty York runs the hotel and he's a friend of Smith's."

"How do you know Salty's there?"

Bonham laughed again, proud of himself. "I kind of tricked Fatty. Soon as the posse left Ganado, I sent a man to Sky City. You see, Smith drank up his money as fast as his pension came in, so I talked him into putting ten dollars in the bank every month for burial money. He didn't want charity, so he's been depositing the ten dollars and drinking up the rest. Well, I sent a note to Fatty York with a hundred dollars, telling him it was Smith's burial money but to use it to take care of him. York took it. That means Smith's there, or York wouldn't have touched it."

"I'd better go see Smith." Kim picked up his hat. "Dunning might make the same guess you did."

"Wouldn't surprise me if he had a man down there already," Bonham said. "If you're goin' to get yourself cleared, it'll be Smith or Martin who does it."

Kim moved to the door, then turned back, smiling a little as he pinned his eyes on Rocky's grave face. "Thanks for everything, Shamrock."

She rose and walked to him, worried but not angry as she usually was when he called her by her name.

"You can't go, Kim," she said in a low, desperate voice. "Not yet."

"I've got to. You helped me buy some time. That's what I needed."

"You haven't bought enough. You might as well have stayed in Ganado."

"No. I'm just sorry you had to risk your neck to save mine."

"Kim," she said, "I wanted to be with you long enough so you'd trust me and know I'm not lying to you."

"I've been with you that long," he said quickly.

She put her hands on his arms, gripping them tightly. "Then believe this. Peg and Dunning aren't fighting. She's in love with him."

There was nothing she could have said that would have shocked him more than that, and he showed it.

"You're mistaken," he said. "You must be."

"No. I've spied on them. I'm not ashamed of it, either. I wouldn't spy on anyone else, but I did on them. Della has, too. There's a place up Ganado Cañon where they meet. We've seen him kiss her. I tell you they're working together."

"What do you think, Brit?" Kim asked.

"Hard to believe," the banker said, "but it explains some things I've wondered about. Dunning's done a lot of talking about busting Clawhammer, but he ain't done much busting."

"But what would it get them?"

"I couldn't say," Bonham said slowly. "There don't seem to be much sense in talking about fighting while they're kissing each other on the side."

"You don't believe me, do you, Kim?" Rocky cried. "You think I'm lying because I hate Peg."

"I just think you're wrong."

"All right," she breathed. "Believe anything you want to, but don't go back to the Clawhammer. Promise me you won't."

"I can't make a promise like that."

199

"Kim, you owe me your life," she whispered, her hands still clutching his arms. "Kim, Kim, don't throw it away. If you go back, you'll never get away alive."

"I'm beholden to you," he said stiffly, "but I can't bind myself by promises. Not even to you."

He pulled his arms away from her hands and left the cabin. Minutes later he rode down the creek, and, as he passed the open door, he saw Rocky sitting at the table, her head on her arms. He went on downslope, an aching emptiness in him. He had talked lightly about not needing a shotgun to marry her, too lightly. Now he knew he loved her.

His thoughts had been muddied up, living close to Peg and thinking he loved her. He was ashamed. Peg had her way of appealing to a man. He would never forget the way she had kissed him, but that kiss had not been prompted by love. Nor could he believe she loved Dunning. It did not seem important either way.

One thought lay in his mind like a smoldering coal. Rocky did not understand why he had refused to make the promise she had asked; she would be thinking he was in love with Peg. So he had built a wall between him and Rocky, and it might be impossible to break through to her again. He rode on down the twisting trail, and the night was very dark around him.

Finally the black mass of the timber was behind him, and he was on the flat with its sagebrush and scattered cedars. Here he left the trail that he and Rocky had followed the night before.

It had not rained that day at Bonham's cabin, but it had rained here, and the air was damp and tangy with sage smell. The sky was still overcast, and along the southern horizon lightning played with quick slashing thrusts that threw a weird light upon a dark earth.

There were no stars to guide him. At times Kim wondered if he was going in the direction he wanted to, for in this pitch blackness a man could easily make a half circle and reverse himself. He thought with grim humor that the lights of Ganado might suddenly appear and he would discover that he was going north instead of south.

He reached the bench and let his buckskin have his head. The animal picked his way down the steep slope, sliding a little in the mud, for apparently the rain had been heavy here. Then he was on the level grassy floor of the valley, and he came, near midnight, to a stream.

Kim reined up, listening, but there was no sound except that of some furtive night animal scurrying among the willows and the distant call of a coyote.

Kim had not expected to run into Dunning and the posse. Distance itself made it unlikely. They would not be in this end of the valley anyhow, if they had gone to Shorty Avis's place. But long experience at this game, both as hunter and hunted, had developed caution in Kim, so he sat his saddle, head turned to catch any sound that might drift in from the level floor of the valley.

He was certain now that he was where he wanted to be. Judging from the size of the stream, this was Pass Creek. It ran almost due south. Somewhere to the north Ganado Creek flowed into Pass Creek. There was no meandering here, for the tilt of the land was greater than north of town. The stream moved with a steady chatter that would become a sullen roar as it churned between the high walls of the cañon before turning west where it would eventually meet the Colorado.

Kim rode downstream, found a break in the willows, and forded the creek. Again he turned south, following the old road that now had little travel, but at one time had known a steady stream of stagecoaches moving between Sky City and Ganado.

Presently the creek dropped below the road that was now a narrow shelf carved out of the cañon wall. A solitary light showed ahead. He reined up again and listened, but heard nothing except the steady hammering of the creek as it spewed in white-foamed fury around the huge boulders in its bed. He rode on, slowly, for he had reached Sky City.

It was a strange town, the cañon dropping away on one side, a sheer sandstone wall rising above it on the other, clinging here on a shelf that was barely wide enough for the buildings and the single street. Kim had been here only once before, but he remembered it well, for Sky City was a town that, once seen, could not easily be forgotten. He pictured it now, the weathered false fronts of the deserted buildings, the long string of cabins with their windows and doors gone and their roofs falling in.

XIV

Fatty York's hotel was the only building still in use in Sky City. He had a small store, a post office, and a bar along with a dining room and the few rooms on the second floor that he rented. Ed Lane made it a rule to stay out of Sky City. It was no place for a sheriff, particularly one like Lane. There were still a few prospectors who haunted the high country and came in twice a year to buy supplies, but the bulk of Fatty York's business was with the toughs who had beaten a posse out of New Mexico.

Kim tied in front of the hotel. There was another horse at the end of the hitch pole. Kim moved toward it, stopped before he reached a patch of light from the hotel windows, and stood studying the horse.

It was possible that the animal belonged to a man on the dodge who had just got in, but in that case the horse would probably have been put in

York's stable. It was Kim's guess that someone planned to ride out soon, possibly an HD man looking for Salty Smith.

From where Kim stood, he could look into the hotel lobby. Fatty York seemed to be dozing behind the desk, his baldhead shiny in the lamplight. No one else was in sight. The bar and dining room were on the other side of the lobby, the interior dark.

Kim went in. York opened his eyes, blinked owlishly, then shook his head as if to clear the cobwebs from his mind.

"Howdy, Logan," he said. "Ain't you off your reservation?"

"Came down to look at the scenery," Kim said.

York laughed. "Scenery, is it? Well, boy, we've got that. Maybe I should advertise."

York was a tall man, but because of his great width he gave the impression of being shorter than he was. He wore a bushy dark mustache that was a sharp contrast with his pale face. Kim had no idea how far the man could be trusted. Bonham considered him honest, but Kim was always skeptical of those who made their living from the owlhoot fringe of society.

"Advertising wouldn't do your business no good, would it?" Kim asked.

York laughed again, taking no offense. "It wouldn't, for a fact. I do purty well, but a man oughta do well, living in this hole." He picked up a half-chewed cigar from the desk and put it into his mouth. "Sky City, population one human being and five thousand ghosts. Funny thing, Logan, how fellers like me and Brit Bonham up there in Ganado hang on, hoping the old camps will come back and knowing they never will. Oughta have our heads examined."

Kim made a quick study of the lobby while York talked. The store and post office were on one side, the door shut and probably locked. The door into the bar was open, a thin finger of light falling into it from the lamp on the desk. An open stairway led to the rooms upstairs. The chances were that the man who owned the other horse was not far away. He might have gone upstairs, or he might be in the bar, listening.

Casually Kim made a slow turn to face the bar door, right hand at his side, left dropped casually on the desk.

"How's business?" he asked.

York laughed as if everything Kim said was funny. "It ain't good, Logan. Too peaceful south of the line. What this country needs is a good bank robbery."

"I don't reckon you'd be interested in keeping a man who's wanted in Colorado?"

"Why, I might." York scratched his blob of a nose, watery eyes fixed on Kim. "For a price. No price, no keep. You savvy that?"

"Sure. I've got the price, all right, and I don't

reckon Ed Lane's likely to be poking his nose down here. He don't want it shot off, Ed don't." Kim leaned against the desk, his mouth close to York's ear. He whispered: "I want to see Salty."

There was no change of expression on York's droopy-cheeked face. "I reckon that's right. Ed sure is a careful gent." He took the cigar out of his mouth, and said in a whisper that barely reached Kim's ears. "Pat Monroney's in the bar."

Kim nodded. Monroney was one of Dunning's gun hands who was fitted for this sort of job. Kim knew him slightly, but even a nodding acquaintance with the man was enough to peg him as a back-shooting killer. He would kill old Salty Smith as casually as he would shoot a prairie dog.

"I don't cotton much to the notion of going on across the line," Kim said. "I like it on this side, but Ganado ain't real healthy for me."

York's big laugh boomed out again. "I heard about that. Well, you'll be as safe here as if you was in church. Good grub three times a day, plenty of whiskey, and a fine bed. Fifty dollars a day."

"Fair enough," Kim said. "Let's have a drink on it. Then I'll see how good that bed of yours is. Been riding so long I wore calluses on my saddle."

This time York didn't laugh. He chewed on the cigar, then said: "Maybe you'd better go on up and start trying the bed. We'll have the drink in the morning."

Monroney appeared in the doorway. "I'll drink with Logan, Fatty. We'll drink to Salty Smith."

York picked up the lamp and waddled into the bar. "All right, only I don't see what you want to drink for at this time of night."

As Kim followed York through the door, Monroney gave him a wink. "Fatty figgers we ain't good pay. Fifty dollars a day is standard rate in this boar's nest. I've had some friends who holed up here. They knock a bank over, take all the risks, then have to give what they've made to this keg of lard who don't do nothing but rustle grub and hand out a bottle of Valley Tan now and then."

"Don't be so smart, friend," York growled sullenly. "Ain't no law making you stay here."

"I ain't staying long." Monroney picked up the bottle and glasses York set on the bar and moved to the table. "Sit down, Logan."

Kim followed, wondering,

Monroney was a knot-headed man with a scarred face and beady eyes set too close together beside a beaky nose. Kim regarded him with high contempt. Tonto Miles or Phil Martin would have come out of the bar with his gun smoking, but Monroney was the sort who avoided danger if he could. It was Kim's guess that he had some kind of a trick up his sleeve that he considered foolproof, or he would have remained under cover.

Monroney poured the drinks and shoved one glass across the table. Kim sat watching Monroney's hands.

"So we're drinking to Salty Smith," he said.

"That's right." Monroney's thin lips held what was meant to be a genial smile. "You know, Logan, you fooled us, which same includes Dunning. We figgered you was just bluff, making all that big talk about the Clawhammer hanging onto every foot of range that old Sam had claimed. Well, Tonto found out how good you are with a six."

Monroney had his drink and put the empty glass down.

"I kind of liked Tonto, but I hear he had his chance. Well, you see how it is. Talk don't really hurt, but if you was smart, you'd get across the line."

Kim waited for the move he knew Monroney planned to make. This was like the man, talking with cool confidence, casually, all the time hoping that Kim's nerves were knotting. There was a moment of silence, broken only by York's heavy breathing behind the bar.

Then Monroney poured another drink and lifted the glass to his mouth, his right hand dropping below the table top. Kim came up out of his chair like a thin spring uncoiling. He heaved the table over on Monroney, his glass and bottle spilling to the floor, and backed away, drawing his .44.

The HD man fell sideward and rolled and came up with his gun. Kim fired, getting Monroney in the chest. Monroney's shot went wide. Kim let go another shot, smashing Monroney's gun arm.

That was all. Monroney lay flat on his back, staring up at Kim and cursing him in a low, wicked tone, the knowledge of death haunting his beady eyes. York came across the room, still breathing hard.

"You ain't smart, Monroney," he said. "Not half as smart as you allowed."

"A man's smart if he makes it." Monroney's left hand gripped his shirt front. He raised his hand and looked at the blood. "He ain't smart if he don't make it. So I ain't smart."

Then, with the last strength that was in him, he grabbed the gun beside him and lifted it. Kim took one quick step and kicked the gun out of Monroney's hand, sending it *clattering* across the floor. Monroney fell back, eyes glazed, blood showing on his lips. He took one hard, sawing breath, then he was still.

"First time I was ever glad to see a man die," York said. "He was fixing to drill you under the table when he took that drink."

"I know," Kim said.

"He got the drop on me," York said bitterly. "I ain't much good with a gun. Don't have to be. The boys all figger they'll need me someday. If Monroney had drilled me, one of 'em would have got him. He should have known that."

Kim moved toward the lobby.

"Come on," he said. "I want to see Salty."

York picked up the lamp and tramped through the door. He set the lamp on the desk and faced Kim, chewing fiercely on a cigar.

"What do you want with him?" he asked.

"He's goin' to answer a question."

"Look, Logan, Salty's a friend of mine." York motioned with a wide inclusive gesture. "I've always been too fat to be good for anything. I mean, like punching cows or working in a mine. Well, I didn't have much money when I came here. Salty staked me to this. Now I'm returning the favor. I'm protecting him. Savvy?"

"I didn't come here to hurt him," Kim said quietly. "It's the other way around. As long as Dunning's riding high around here, Salty's in a tight. If I can keep my neck out of a rope long enough, I'll get Dunning. Then Salty can go home."

Still York hesitated. "It ain't that simple," he finally said. "I don't know what's going on up the valley, but I do know you're with the Clawhammer. Why don't you go back and do your fighting where you oughta?"

"They want me for a killing," Kim answered. "I can't do no fighting till I clean that up. Salty can do it for me."

"How do you figger Salty knows anything?"

"He wouldn't be here if he didn't know who killed Yuma Bill." Sweat broke out on the fat man's face. Kim, sensing the agony of uncertainty that was in him, said patiently: "I told you I wasn't here to hurt the old man, York. I aim to do him a favor as well as myself."

"All right," York said. "I'll go get him, but if you lay a hand on him, I'll black your name from here to Hades."

York started up the stairs, the steps *creaking* under his great weight. Kim followed.

"Stay there!" York called back over his shoulder. "I told you I'd get him."

"I'll tag along."

York turned, holding the lamp high, its light falling across Kim's dark, stubble-covered face. "My word goes around here. Savvy?"

"You could get him out while I waited."

"Blast it, I . . ."

"Ever feel a rope on your neck?" Kim asked.

"No."

"I've got one waiting for me in Ganado if I let Salty get away from me. Now go on."

York went on. Reaching the hall, he lumbered along it to the back room. He tapped on the door, calling: "Salty!"

"What's wrong?" the old man quavered.

York pushed the door open and went in. "Nothing now, Salty. Everything's all right." He set the lamp on the bureau. "There was plenty wrong a while ago. Monroney was here, aiming to make me tell him where you was, but Logan came in and drilled him."

Smith was eyeing Kim in abject fear. "Go away, Logan!" he cried out. "I don't know nothing."

"Logan ain't here to hurt you, Salty," York said, "but Monroney would have if Logan hadn't got him. You owe him something, so you'd best tell him what he wants to know."

Smith looked down at the floor. "I don't know nothing."

"You know who killed Yuma Bill," Kim said. "Dunning wants to hang me for it."

Smith's gnarled hands fisted. He sat on the edge of the bed, a dirty-bearded old man smelling of stale sweat and cheap whiskey. Kim found it hard to believe he had once been a wealthy man and one of the town fathers of Ganado.

"I don't know nothing," Smith repeated, still staring at the floor.

"You want to go back home," York urged. "Only way to fix it so you can is to tell Logan."

"He won't fix nothing!" Smith shrilled. "Logan's a Clawhammer man. He'll kill me. Monroney didn't have nothing against me."

"You're wrong, Salty," York said patiently. "You've got to believe me when I tell you Monroney would have killed me and you both. He's the one who wanted to shut your mouth."

Kim crossed the room and sat down beside Smith. "Phil Martin claims I did it. You and me know different. I'm not working for the Clawhammer any more. That makes a lot of difference, Salty."

"You're lying."

"No, Peg fired me. Bonham helped bust me out of jail. Bonham's your friend, too."

"A good friend," Smith whispered. "It's you I don't know about. I figgered you'd kill me if I talked."

"No," Kim said with the patience he would have used with a child, "it's Dunning's bunch that wants to kill you. I've got to clear myself. Then I can help you."

Smith turned bloodshot eyes to York. "I'd like to go home, Fatty. I'd like to go home."

"Tell him," York urged. "It ain't like we figgered, or Monroney wouldn't have come here tonight."

"All right, I'll tell him." Smith's hands gripped his knees. "I was fishing. See? I was just above my cabin a piece. I had a bite and I was trying to get that trout out from under a willow when I heard a shot. I looked up. One feller was on the ground. This other feller had a smoking gun in his hand. He stooped down and yanked off the dead man's money belt."

"Who was it?" Kim asked.

Smith drew back, suspicion clouding his mind

again. "You're a Clawhammer. I don't trust you."

"I'm not working for the Clawhammer," Kim told him again, "but it wouldn't make any difference if I was. You see, Monroney wouldn't have been here to shut your mouth if it had been a Clawhammer man who killed Yuma Bill."

"But I saw what I saw!" Smith shouted. "It was a Clawhammer, I tell you. It was . . . it was . . ." He turned his eyes to York. "Get me a drink, Fatty. Seems like I can't remember nothing."

"No drink," Kim said, impatience crowding him. "Not till he answers my question."

"It . . ." Smith got up. "It was . . ." He backed across the room, watching Kim with worried uncertainty. Then he blurted: "It was Dutch Heinz."

Kim forgot to breathe. He had the same feeling that he'd had when Rocky had told him Peg was in love with Dunning. It didn't seem possible that Dutch Heinz had killed Yuma Bill, not with Dunning and Martin trying to protect the killer. Then he remembered other things—Heinz's wanting to rob Yuma Bill that night in Peg's kitchen, Peg's pressing need for money, Yuma Bill's saying he had heard someone ride out of the yard. Kim still didn't have all the threads, but he had enough to form the pattern. Dunning and Heinz and Peg were together.

"Surprised?" York asked.

"Plenty."

Kim got up from the bed, watching Salty Smith who had backed against the wall and was staring at him with the soul-deep fear of a man who thinks he may still be killed.

"What are you goin' to do?" York asked.

"Can't let Smith go back," Kim said thoughtfully. "Too dangerous. You'll have to keep him for a while. Till you get word that Dunning's finished. Then he can go home. You fetch that bottle and bring up a pen and paper. Salty's gonna write out a statement of what he saw, and I'll shove it down Ed Lane's throat."

"The way I heard it, Martin claimed you . . ."

"You heard right," Kim said, "but now that I know who did beef Yuma Bill, Martin's goin' to change his story." Kim jerked his head at the door. "Go get that bottle. Salty deserves it."

XV

Mid-morning found Kim in Ganado. He was sleepy and hungry and more tired than he had ever been before in his life. Still, food and sleep must wait. He had no way of knowing where the posse was, but by this time every member would be worn to a frazzle.

The question in Kim's mind was whether the posse had returned to town. Ed Lane had probably caught up with Dunning and the others. The trick would be to get Lane and Phil Martin together. If Kim could do that, he was reasonably sure he could clear himself.

Kim rode into town on a side street that was flanked by deserted houses. The entire town seemed as empty of life as the empty buildings facing the street. Ed Lane lived in a white house one block east of the courthouse. Kim turned into an alley and came to the rear of the sheriff's home. The only sign of life was the column of smoke rising from the chimney. Dismounting, Kim led his buckskin into Lane's barn and left him where he would not be seen by anyone passing. Lane's horse was in a stall, and, judging from his appearance, he had been ridden long and hard.

Kim walked to the back door, hoping that Lane would be inside. He knocked, and Lane's housekeeper opened the door. Kim shoved past her into the house.

"I want to see Lane," he said

"You can't force your way into a house like this," the woman said in a strident voice. "Ed will arrest you for breaking and entering. Now get out before I call him."

"I've already entered, and I'll sure break something if I don't see Ed. Where is he?"

The woman backed away toward the stove, apparently afraid. "You . . . you're Kim Logan, ain't you?"

"That's right. Where's Lane?"

"You've come here to kill . . . ?"

"Shut up. I'm not going to hurt you. Or Ed, if he behaves, but I don't figure on standing here all morning asking you where he is."

"He's asleep. He just got in a little while ago."

"Looks like he'll be waking up *pronto*. Which room?"

She kept backing away until she stood with her back against the sink. "Don't you come no closer! Don't you lay a hand on me."

The woman was a middle-aged blonde, as dumpy as a filled wool sack.

"You're exaggerating your talents, ma'am," Kim said mildly. "Ed's the one I want. Now unless you want him hurt, you stay right there, peaceful-like."

He stepped into the living room. One door opened into the parlor; the door on the other side of the room was closed. Kim opened it and looked in. It was Lane's bedroom. He lay crosswise on the bed in the manner of a man who had fallen there and gone to sleep at once, too tired to move. He had not even bothered to undress. Only his coat, Stetson, and gun belt were on the chair beside the bed.

Kim pulled the chair back so Lane could not reach his gun. Then he put up the blind and the morning sunshine cut squarely across the sheriff's face.

"Time to get up and start the day, Ed," Kim said, shaking Lane.

The sheriff gave a great gurgling snore, and kept on sleeping. Kim shook him again, with considerable violence, and Lane reared up, eyes blinking in the sunlight.

"No sense sleeping all day, Ed," Kim said. "Time to get up."

Recognition struck Lane then, and his eyes became bright with fear. His face and the front of his shiny baldhead turned white. He let out a hoarse yelp, both hands reaching out in a wild grab for his gun. The chair wasn't where he had left it, and he fell out of bed, hitting the floor with a great *clatter* and shaking a picture on the wall above him.

"Now what do you know about that?" Kim stood with one foot on a chair rung, a hand dropped on the gun belt dangling over the back. "Somebody moved that chair."

Lane sat up, rubbed his eyes, and shook his head.

"What do you want?" he blurted.

"Heard you was looking for me, so I came in. You don't seem real pleased about it."

"Sure, sure. You're showing sense now. Too bad Bonham didn't show as much when he helped bust you out. I'll have him and that Della Naylor keeping you company behind bars 'fore the day's over."

Lane got to his feet and started toward the chair. He stopped abruptly when Kim held up a hand.

"You don't need your gun. I've got a surprise for you. I didn't plug Yuma Bill."

"You've said that before, but a jury . . ."

"We don't even need a jury." Kim pulled a folded piece of paper from his pocket and held it up for Lane to see, then replaced it. "I've got a statement signed by an eyewitness. You know, Ed, it's goin' to be real dangerous, bringing in that *hombre* that beefed Yuma Bill."

"I won't have to go far," Lane flung at him. "Not with you standing right here, and I'll have Bonham . . ."

"Did you see Bonham help me out of jail?"

"Somebody slugged me when Della . . ."

Lane stopped, red-faced. Kim laughed.

"You sure made a fool out of yourself. What do you think Johnny's goin' to do when you tell folks you got slugged when you was kissing his wife?" Kim shook his head. "You'd better keep mum. Ed, you do what I want you to and I'll keep still about you and Del. I'll be saving your life. Johnny sure is a jealous *hombre*."

"All right. What do you want?"

"We'll take a walk to Doc's place and see Phil Martin. I've got a notion he'll change his yarn."

For a moment Lane stood there, blinking idiotically, unable to find a way out.

"Gimme my coat," he said sourly. "I need a chaw of tobacco."

Kim tossed the coat to Lane who slipped into it, took a plug of tobacco out of his pocket, and gnawed off a mouthful.

"Gimme my gun belt," he said thickly. "I'd look naked without it."

Kim lifted the gun from holster and removed the shells, then handed the belt and gun to Lane.

"You had your fun pushing me down the street the other day. Now I'll have some. Don't load that iron. Walk out ahead of me and keep going till we get to Doc's drugstore."

Lane swore, but he obeyed. As he crossed the living room, his housekeeper called: "What's he doing to you, Ed?"

"Nothing. We've got some business to attend to."

When they were outside, Kim said: "I thought the posse rode off and left you."

"I caught up with 'em at the Clawhammer. I figgered you'd go there."

"Where's Dunning and his outfit?"

"They stopped at the Clawhammer. Dunning stayed there, and the rest of us came back to town. Johnny had to go out on the stage, and Luke Haines allowed he'd better get back to see how his wife was."

"Ain't it funny Dunning would stop at the Clawhammer?"

"Looked funny to me," Lane admitted, "but they all needed sleep, Dunning said."

They walked in silence then, Kim thinking that this was further proof of what Rocky had said about Peg and Dunning. They turned into the drugstore. Doc Frazee stood behind the counter, looking tired and sleepy, and even surprise at seeing Kim did not change the expression on his bony face.

"Well, Ed, I see you caught your man," Frazee said. "Shall we hang him this morning, or wait till Dunning gets back to town?"

Lane glowered, saying nothing. "Got anything for a sour disposition, Doc?" Kim said.

"Sure, but you can get it cheaper in the Belle Union."

"Come on," Lane said irritably. "Get on with the business."

"How's Martin?" Kim asked.

"Purty sick. The fool should have stayed in bed, but, no, he figured he was so tough he didn't need to do what he was told."

"I want to see him," Kim said. "He's goin' to tell who beefed Yuma Bill. I've got a statement from Salty Smith, so I figured, if Martin's story jibes with Smith's, even Lane will get it through his noggin that I ain't the man he wants."

Frazee stood motionlessly for a moment, stroking his goatee. "Let me handle this, Kim," he finally said. "I've got a scheme I've been waiting to use till Ed was here to listen."

221

The medico led the way to a side room, motioning for Kim and Lane to wait outside the door.

"How do you feel, Phil?" they heard him ask.

"I'm burning up," Martin groaned.

"They tell me Hades is hot, too. I reckon you'll be finding out before long, but it might ease your conscience if you'd tell me who drilled Yuma Bill."

"I'm sick," Martin grunted, "but I ain't sick enough to admit I'm a liar."

Frazee put a hand on Martin's forehead and jerked it away. "I could fry an egg right there, Phil. I'll stir up something to take your fever down."

Frazee poured water into a glass, dropped a spoonful of white powder into it, and stirred lustily.

"Here, Phil. Drink this."

Frazee got a hand behind Martin's head and Martin emptied the glass.

"Phil," Frazee said, "there's time when a sawbones has to stick his nose into business that ain't rightfully his. That's just what I've done. Logan didn't beef that *hombre*. You know who did. The way I see it, that makes you guilty of killing if Logan hangs, but there ain't no court hereabouts that'll see justice done. So I took care of it myself."

"What're you driving at?"

"I executed you. That was poison you just drank. Tasted awful, didn't it? In about a minute you'll feel a tingling in your fingers and toes. Then it'll be in your hands and feet. Pretty soon it'll go up into your arms and legs. When it hits your heart, *wham,* you're dead."

"You're lying."

"Think so? Well, I wish I had Hank Dunning here so I could lie to him the same way."

"Do something, cuss it!" Martin cried. "You can't just stand there and let me die!"

"Getting into your legs, ain't it? It'll be up in your arms. First they tingle, then they'll get stiff. Pretty soon . . ."

Martin lifted himself on his one good arm, yelling: "Shut up, and do something!"

"You'll make your fever worse, carrying on thataway," Frazee said reprovingly. He took a bottle down from a shelf and filled a small glass with amber liquid. "This is the antidote, Phil. I aim to get the truth out of you or kill you. Tell me who drilled Yuma Bill and you get the antidote."

"Go to the devil," Martin breathed, and fell back.

"I didn't think you were that big a fool," Frazee said contemptuously. "You're lying to get rid of Logan, and you're doing it because Dunning told you to. Now ain't that a fine thing to die for?"

"Go to the devil!" Martin said again.

"You're the one going to the devil. My

conscience won't hurt me for sending you there. I'm trying to save an innocent man's life. Do you think that what Dunning told you to do is enough to kill yourself for? Getting it in your legs and arms now, aren't you? When it hits your heart . . ."

"All right!" Martin screamed. "It was Heinz."

"Now that's better. Here's your . . ."

"Wait a minute," Kim called from outside the door. "Did Dutch get the money?"

"Sure, sure. Hank and that Cody woman rigged it. She said he'd have all the *dinero* in a shoe box. Forty thousand. Said the old gent was gonna keep the *dinero* while you rode into town, but you fooled 'em when you took the box. Dutch couldn't find it, so he figured the old man had the *dinero* on him. That's how he found the money belt. Now gimme that stuff, Doc."

"Here you are," Frazee said.

Martin hoisted himself up on his good arm and drained the glass.

"Whiskey!" he yelled. "Nothing but cheap whiskey." He threw the glass against the wall. "You lying son-of-a-bitch! When I get out of here, I'll . . ."

"Cool down, boy," Frazee said. "That's no way to act after my saving your life. Whiskey is a good antidote for a lot of things."

Frazee walked out, leaving Martin staring after him, uncertain whether he had been tricked or not. The medico shut the door, winking at Kim.

"If properly used, bicarbonate of soda and imagination can do more to change men's lives than all the pills a doctor can roll."

Kim handed Smith's statement to Frazee. "You know Salty Smith's handwriting, Doc?"

"Sure. Nobody could forget that old fool's scrawling. Not even a barnyard hen." He glanced at the paper and, nodding, handed it to Lane. "It tallies, Ed."

Lane studied the paper, then glanced up at Kim. "Where is Smith?"

"He's safe. You go get Dutch. Salty'll be here to testify at his trial."

"Where is he?" Lane asked again.

"I wouldn't trust you as far as I could throw you by the hair on your head," Kim said bluntly. "If Smith was dead, Martin could go back on his story, so I aim to keep Smith alive."

Lane wheeled toward the door. Frazee called: "Ed!"

Lane faced the medico, glowering at him.

"Ed," Frazee said, "you're a tinhorn politician. We all know that, but if you haven't got the nerve it takes to go after Dutch Heinz, you'd better turn in your star."

"I don't get it!" Lane shouted. "Heinz has been with the Clawhammer ever since Sam Cody drove into the valley. It don't make sense that Dunning would protect him and try to hang Logan."

"I'm not working for the Clawhammer," Kim said in a low tone.

"I still don't savvy."

"You don't need to savvy. Are you going after Heinz?"

Lane stood in the doorway, trembling. "I'll go look for him," he muttered.

"You'd better find him," Frazee said. "Things are changing around here. A few more funerals will just about clean things up."

When Lane left the drugstore, Kim said: "He's a dead man if he goes after Heinz."

"Or a man without a job if he don't," Frazee said. "He can't make up his mind which way to jump."

Kim walked to the door and yawned.

"Guess I'll get some breakfast and sleep till Christmas. Thanks, Doc. I'm so near all in I ain't got it through my noggin that I don't have to keep ducking the law."

"No need to thank me, Kim." Frazee's bony face was grave. "You know, the other morning, when I was standing in front of the bank, I wasn't much different from Fred Galt and Luke Haines. Kind of felt that the country had gone to the dogs and I didn't give a hoot. Then you fetched in that *dinero* and, well, things began looking different."

"Yuma Bill was the one who made things look different," Kim said.

"To you," Frazee agreed. "It's like a chain. But

it was some different with me. I'd been rotting inside for years. I'd seen this country boom and I'd seen it die. I've seen a few honest folks and a lot of crooked ones. Why, if I could collect all the money I've got coming, I'd be a rich man. I've got enough, though. The thing was I got to talking to Brit about what the country used to be like. We want to see it come back and I think it will. Trouble is, it ain't good for folks to live with ghosts. A lot of us have been gripped by the dead hand of the past till we've been paralyzed."

"It ain't the dead hand of the past that's been bothering me," Kim said, and left the medico's office.

He had flapjacks at the Chinese restaurant, then, taking his horse out of Lane's barn, rode to the livery stable. It was a grim sort of joke, he thought, that he had cheated the lynch mob by riding out of town on Shorty Avis's black, for Shorty hated him with only a little less bitterness than Hank Dunning did. He told the stableman to keep the gelding until Shorty or Rocky came for him, stopped to talk to his buckskin, and left the stable.

Kim went to the bank. What Doc Frazee had said about being gripped by the dead hand of the past had given him an idea. Charlie Bemis froze behind the teller's wicket when he saw Kim.

"You loco, Kim?" he blurted. "The posse just got back this morning. They'll . . ."

227

"No, they won't. I'm goin' to laugh in Fred Galt's face soon as I get some sleep. Brit back yet?"

Bemis nodded. "He's in his office. Lane . . ."

"He don't want me," Kim said. Stepping through the gate at the end of the counter, he walked on back to Bonham's office. He knocked, and opened the door at the banker's: "Come in."

"Don't get excited, Brit," he said. "The law don't want me. Charlie had himself a conniption when I came in."

XVI

Paling when he saw who had come in, Bonham had started to get up. Then he dropped back into his chair, his body going slack, and it seemed to Kim that his shoulders were more stooped than ever.

"Let's hear the yarn before I die of heart failure," Bonham said, filling his pipe, his eyes dropping to his tobacco pouch.

Kim told him what had happened. "What about Rocky?" he asked then.

"She lit out for home. Mighty worried about you, too. You'd best ride out there as soon as you get some sleep."

"I aim to." Kim canted his chair back against

the wall and rolled a smoke. "What do you want most, Brit?"

Bonham lit his pipe, blinking at the smoke. He took the pipe stem out of his mouth. "Now what a question."

"Sure is," Kim agreed. "Maybe it's because I'm so sleepy that my head's spinning, but I think I've got an idea. Strikes me that some of you old-timers, you and Doc, for instance, want to see this country come back before you go over the range."

"That's right," Bonham said, "but who's goin' to bring it back? I've got a little claim up there back of my cabin, but it ain't no bonanza. Same with Doc."

"Mines come and go, Brit. Trouble with you and Doc is you saw this country when it had its boom, so you figure that another strike is the only way to bring it back. You're wrong, Brit. The grass will always be here."

Bonham gestured impatiently. "We've had cows in this valley ever since Sam Cody brought his herd in. Before that even, but it didn't bring no big prosperity."

"And I'll tell you why. The Clawhammer and the HD are both big outfits. It's the little fry who'll bring the country back, fellows like Shorty Avis. If this range was handled right, there'd be enough grass for fifty outfits. It means business for everybody, more'n you'd ever have with two big spreads and a few dinky ones on the mesa."

Bonham shook his head. "There's a gent named Hank Dunning . . ."

Kim's face was bone-hard. "I'll attend to Dunning, and I'll attend to Heinz if Lane don't."

"You've been a fool for luck," Bonham said, "although I've always claimed it takes a real good man to have good luck. You might pull it off, but no matter what happens to Dunning, there's still Peg."

"You've got her notes."

"Yeah, and it won't hurt my conscience to close her out after what's happened." Bonham studied his pipe, eyes almost lidded shut. "But I had the notion you were in love with Peg."

Kim's face reddened. "I guess Rocky called it right. I was in love with the Clawhammer, not Peg. It's Rocky I'm in love with, and I'll prove it to her if I have to stay here a million years."

"Might take that long. It's my guess Rocky's goin' to be hard to convince."

"I'll do it if it takes that million years. Now you've got forty thousand dollars you don't know what to do with. My idea is for you to loan it out to the little fry. Let 'em start in the valley again. If we don't have talk of a range war, there'll be others who'll move in."

Bonham leaned back, puffing steadily, eyes on the ceiling. "You're dreaming, boy, just dreaming. There's a lot to be done before what you're talking about can be anything but dreams."

"We'll do 'em."

"Kim," Bonham said slowly, "you've always been a fiddle-footed drifter. How do I know you've changed?"

Kim got up. "You don't. Go ahead and keep Yuma's money in your safe, but I'm betting that, when you go over the range, Yuma will be standing beside Saint Peter and he'll blackball you before you get through the Pearly Gates."

Kim would have stalked out if Bonham hadn't said: "That might happen. I'll make you a deal. Interested?"

"Maybe," Kim answered, turning back.

"A lot of things can change a man," Bonham said, "but a woman's the best. That's how it was with Yuma. Like I told you, he was mighty ornery once. Bought a big grant in New Mexico and sold land to settlers that wasn't no good for farming. They failed and moved on and the land went back to him. Then he sold it over again. He piled up a lot of money, then he fell in love with one of them farmers' girls, and she made him into the Yuma Bill you knew. By that time he couldn't give the money back to the fellers he'd taken it from, so he came up to the Arkansas Valley and did his blamedest to help other people with that money. Kim, what you've said is right in line with what Yuma Bill would want done with his money. Even after his wife died, he went right on like he had been. If you'd marry Peg, you wouldn't be no different than when you rode into the valley, but if it's Rocky you marry, you'll be different. I'll gamble on that."

"What's your deal?" Kim asked in a dry tone.

"The day you marry Rocky, I'll loan that forty thousand dollars."

"You've made a deal," Kim said, and left the bank.

He was as angry as he could be at a man who had helped save his life, but he could not remain angry at Brit Bonham. The banker had always been the little ranchers' friend; he was Rocky's friend. If his and Bonham's positions had been reversed, he would have figured on the future exactly as the banker had.

Kim took a room and climbed the stairs, thinking of Rocky. Without her, his future would be little different from his past, not the kind of future he wanted. He pulled off his coat and gun belt, tossed his Stetson on the bureau, and fell across the bed. His last thought was of Rocky.

It was dark when Kim awoke. His door was open and a thin pencil of light from the bracket lamp in the hall fell half across his room. He wasn't sure what had wakened him, but he thought someone was shaking him and talking to him. He turned toward the wall, hoping he was dreaming.

No dream. It came again, a slender hand on his shoulder, shaking him with nagging insistence.

A woman's voice beat against his sleep-numbed brain.

"Wake up, Kim! Wake up!"

He sat up, knuckling his eyes and shaking his head. Then he saw Della Naylor.

"Howdy, Del," he mumbled. "Thought you was a dream."

"And I thought you were dead. Are you awake enough to listen?"

"Sure," Kim said, suddenly conscious of the urgency in her voice. "What's wrong?"

"Everything, Kim. The Avis place was burned last night and Shorty Avis was beaten up. Doc's on his way out there now, but I'm afraid he's too late."

Kim swung his feet to the floor, brain as numb as if he had been struck on the head. This was a nightmare. It had to be. When he had cleared himself of Yuma Bill's death, he had thought the immediate problem had been taken care of. Arresting Dutch Heinz was the sheriff's responsibility, and that, Kim had supposed, was the only other chore that needed to be done at once. Now, staring at Della's worried face, he knew that the worst fears of the mesa ranchers would soon be realized. This blow at Shorty Avis was meant as an example of what would happen to the rest if they didn't get out of the country. Kim buckled on his gun belt.

"Who did it?" he asked.

"We don't know. Shorty's unconscious. When

Rocky went home from Bonham's cabin, she found her dad. Everything they own is gone except their cattle."

"They'll lose their beef, too," Kim said somberly, "unless something happens to change Dunning's mind."

Kim put on his hat and coat and turned to the door.

"Kim!" Della cried.

He swung back to face her. "What?"

"Rocky doesn't know I'm here. I came to get Doc and he told me you'd found out about Heinz. I got to wondering what you'd do. There's nothing to hold you in the valley now that you've lost your job with the Clawhammer."

It was natural enough for her to think that. Probably her father, Abe Fawcett, and the rest of the mesa ranchers would think the same thing. He was a gunslinger, and, when he lost his job, he'd ride on. A year ago he would have done exactly that. He might have a week ago. But as Doc Frazee said, the events of the last few days formed a chain going back to Yuma Bill who had owed a debt to Brit Bonham. When Kim had delivered the money, Bonham had owed a debt. Now Kim owed a debt to Della Naylor and Rocky Avis. That would have been enough to make him stay even if he had not loved Rocky.

"I've got another job to do," Kim said. "I aim to hang around a while."

She came toward him, the faint light from the hall touching her troubled face. He had never supposed she had a serious thought in her rattle-brained head. When she had married Johnny Naylor, folks said they were two of a kind, reckless and wild, and they belonged together. But Della had changed, just as everything on this range was changing, for people and their relationships were distorted by the gods of evil that had been loosed upon the valley when Hank Dunning and Peg Cody had opened Pandora's box. Now Kim wondered whether Della and Johnny did belong together. She had grown up and Johnny had lagged behind.

"There's another thing, Kim," Della said. "Yesterday Heinz saw every rancher on the east mesa. He's giving us till sunset tomorrow to get out."

"He gave Shorty a warning like that the other day."

She nodded. "Sam Cody drove us out of the valley, and Heinz thinks he can drive us off the mesa just as easy. He said, if we wanted to sell, to be in town tomorrow afternoon and Peg would buy our land and cattle. If we didn't, we wouldn't get anything."

Kim turned toward the door again, saying: "Come on."

She followed him along the hall, down the stairs, and outside.

"Where are we going?" she asked.

"That's the craziest question I ever heard," he said. "We're going up on the mesa and get your neighbors together. If they want to run, there's nothing anybody can do for 'em, but if they want to fight, we'll show Dutch Heinz a thing or two."

"They won't run, Kim," she said with grim certainty. "They've had one meeting . . . the night after Shorty had his warning. They saw this coming."

"Then we'll fight."

"It's not as simple as that, Kim. Rocky and I believe in you. So does Doc Frazee and Brit Bonham. But to Dad and the rest, you're still Peg Cody's snake stomper."

"Then we'll have to do some arguing," he said.

They took the stage road out of town, keeping a steady, ground-eating pace. Within the hour they reached the road that led to Indian Springs. It was little more than a trail. Beyond the Avis and Fawcett places it climbed to the top of the slick rock rim through a narrow break and ran on through the aspens and spruce to join the stage road just west of the pass. Kim had followed the upper end of this road when he had brought Yuma Bill to the Avis place.

The bulk of the mesa ranchers lived north of the stage road, for that part of the mesa had the best grass, and it was natural that they would go there when Sam Cody had driven them out of the valley. This sudden and violent move on Heinz's part must have been supported by Dunning.

It was Kim's guess that Dunning and his tough crew had been with Heinz when Shorty Avis was beaten and his buildings burned. There could be but one answer. Kim's thoughts came back to the same place they had been many times since Rocky had told him that Peg and Dunning were in love. At least they had thrown in together and were planning a big expansion of their herds. Only a frantic need for more summer range would explain a raid like this.

The country south of Ganado Cañon was not used by any of the ranchers, for it was poor graze all the way to the New Mexico line where it became a maze of impenetrable gorges. As it stood now, the Clawhammer was obliged to seek summer range in the high country between the mesa and the Divide where the season was comparatively short. In the past it had been sufficient because the Clawhammer beef had been held in the valley most of the year, but the valley grass would not be enough if the Clawhammer herd was doubled.

It seemed incredible, but it must be this way. The much-talked about fight between the Clawhammer and the HD had been faked, a smoke screen to hide Peg's and Dunning's real intent. A few shots had been fired across the creek; there had been a good deal of maneuvering when the two outfits had hit Ganado the same day. Supposedly Kim's reputation had held Dunning back, but all the time Peg had known Dunning would not make a serious attack. That was why she had been so sure she would be safe when she stayed at home with no one to protect her but old Limpy.

At last logic forced Kim to the conclusion that his pride had kept him from reaching before. He had been a tool, a small but essential cog in Peg's scheming. It was the reason she had hired him; it was the reason she had paid him the high wages she had.

There were still some facts that Kim did not have and he needed them to bring the muddled pattern out clearly, but this much he could no longer doubt. She had told him she was ambitious; she aimed to be big, so big that the valley would be hers. She had said that when she needed the mesa, the little ranchers would go. Her time of need, he thought grimly, must have come quickly after his talk with her the night he had brought Yuma Bill to the Clawhammer. Apparently Yuma's coming had forced Peg and Dunning into the open. They had planned to steal his money. That was why Phil Martin and his men had crossed the creek. It was why Peg told Heinz that Yuma Bill would be at Smith's cabin with the money. There it was, as plain and brutal a pattern of robbery and killing as Kim had ever seen. A man could not have fooled him, but Peg Cody had, for the simple reason that he had wanted to believe in her.

One thing still bothered Kim. Doubling the Clawhammer and the HD herds would take money. The ten thousand Dutch Heinz had stolen from Yuma Bill would not be enough. They must hold another trump card they had not played, or they wouldn't have started pushing the mesa ranchers as soon as they had.

It was after midnight when Kim and Della reached the bench. They climbed the steep pitch to the mesa, and pulled up to blow their horses.

"If you knew the law didn't want me and you thought there was nothing here to hold me," Kim asked, "how come you bothered to wake me up?"

"I had to be sure," she answered. "Rocky and I invested quite a bit in you. I guess Rocky had her own reasons, but mine were pretty simple. I just figured that, when the chips were down, you'd have to be on our side."

"I won't be much help if your bunch won't trust me," he said wryly.

"That worried me more than anything else." Leather *squeaked* as Della shifted her weight. "There's something else, too. Take me. I know what folks have said. I'm as wild as a March wind and reckless and a little crazy. Johnny's the same, so the old gossips say we'll have the meanest kids in the country." She laughed softly. "Well, maybe we will. Right now I'm awful mad at Johnny, but I'll get over it. When he gets back from his stage run, we'll have a fight and I'll call him terrible names, but after that we'll make up and it will be wonderful. I love him, Kim. No matter what he does, I'll still love him. Don't ask me to explain why. I guess it's just the way a woman's heart works, and you can't explain that."

They rode on across the mesa, through the sage and the scattered black dots that were the wind-shaped cedars, and Kim's thoughts were as dark as the night that pressed down around them. Della had been talking about her heart, but she had been really trying to tell him about Rocky's. Rocky must have loved him for a long time. When he had needed help, she had been there. Kim Logan was not a praying man, but he prayed now, riding through the night with the wind on his face and cold brilliant stars above him, prayed that the knowledge of his love for Rocky had not come too late.

XVII

Climbing steadily now, they reached the pines, not far north of the tableland where Kim and Yuma Bill had fought Phil Martin and his bunch. Then, with dawn not more than an hour away, they reached Abe Fawcett's place. The windows were bright with lamplight.

"Keep your temper, Kim," Della said, "no matter what happens. Maybe I made a mistake bringing you. I mean, Dad and Ma and the rest of them up here have been afraid of the Clawhammer so long they're going to be hard to convince about you."

"I know," he said, "but that ain't worrying me as much as the time. It's goin' to take all day to get 'em together."

"They'll be at the Avis clearing a little before sunup," she told him.

As they reined up in front of the house, the front door opened and Della's mother stood there, a rifle in her hands.

"Who is it?" she called.

"Me," Della answered. "Kim Logan's with me."

"Logan!" Mrs. Fawcett came down the path, Winchester held on the ready. "You get out of here! Shorty Avis is lying in my bed right now looking like he's going over the range, and you've got the brass . . ."

"It wasn't Kim that done it," Della cut in. "He's on our side."

"Our side!" Mrs. Fawcett cried in rage. "Maybe he can pull the wool over your eyes, but he don't fool me. Now you get out of here, Logan, and . . ."

"Then I'll go, too," Della said quietly. "So will Rocky. Doc here?"

"He's working on Shorty now. Della, we don't need this double-crossing gunslinger. If he's on our side, which I doubt, he'll want pay and we haven't got it to give him. I don't trust a man who fights for money, and I wouldn't trust Kim Logan anyhow."

"You don't understand, Ma. A lot has happened the last few days. Everything's changed. Doc will tell you that."

Mrs. Fawcett sniffed. "Everything's changed, has it? Nothing changes. You slap some paint on a tiger and you make him look different, but the stripes are still there. Same with a skunk."

Looking down at Mrs. Fawcett, Kim could not make out the expression on her face, but her hostility was a tangible pressure laid against him. Kim had a feeling that it would take little to make Mrs. Fawcett start shooting. If she did, no one on the mesa but Rocky and her own daughter would condemn her.

He had to work on her pride. It was the only weapon he could use, the same weapon he must use later when he faced Abe Fawcett and the rest of the mesa ranchers.

"A skunk has his way of fighting, ma'am," he said evenly. "But you take a band of sheep now. They just run."

He heard her gasp as if he'd knocked the wind out of her. She would give ground or she'd shoot. The younger ones like Rocky and Della did not remember, but the older ones, men and women both, would remember and be ashamed. Fear would be in them again when the time came that they must make the decision to fight or run, and all the tough talk in the world could not hide it.

"I suppose you think a skunk can protect sheep?" she said harshly.

"He can if he makes enough smell."

Stepping down, Kim walked past Mrs. Fawcett and went into the house. A moment before she had been capable of shooting him in the back, but he knew he had won now. He heard the hum of talk between Della and her mother, then he was in the house.

The Fawcett house was a rambling, two-story structure built of logs, the most pretentious place on the mesa. The front room took up half of the lower floor. At one end an open stairway led to the bedrooms overhead; a cavernous stone fireplace occupied almost all of the other end. Its furniture was homemade and crude, the rough plank floor bare. Kim had the feeling that the Fawcetts had hoped to hold a little of their past glory by building this huge house.

The kitchen formed one back quarter of the first floor, a bedroom the other quarter. The bedroom door was ajar, and Kim pushed it open and went in. Rocky stood at one side of the bed, Doc Frazee on the other. Shorty Avis lay motionless, a faded quilt pulled up under his chin. His head was bandaged, and his face was a mass of cuts and bruises.

Rocky turned, giving Kim a tired smile. Frazee snapped his bag shut.

"Nothing more I can do. He may come out of it. Can't tell yet. Just keep him quiet."

Frazee walked out. Kim stood beside Rocky, and looked down at Shorty's battered face. Shorty Avis was the one man on the mesa who would have stood and fought. That was the reason he had been picked.

"I'm sorry," Kim said, realizing how utterly inadequate the words were.

He put an arm around Rocky. She buried her face against his shirt, crying softly. It was the first sign of weakness he had ever seen in her. She regained control of herself almost at once. She wiped her eyes and looked up at him, trying to smile.

"I'm glad Della let you know," she said. "Thanks for coming."

"No need to thank me," he said.

He looked at Shorty's battered face, anger beginning to burn in him. This was too much. A man under any circumstances had the right to a fair fight. They had not given Shorty Avis that, or any part of it.

"You see why I hate Peg Cody," Rocky breathed. "We knew this would happen after

Dutch Heinz brought us that warning, but we didn't think it would be this soon."

He made no effort to defend Peg. "I'll square this, Rocky," he said. "That's a promise."

"Squaring it won't save Dad."

"It may save some others."

She moved away from him, her shoulders slack as if all the weariness and worry and fear that had crowded her for so long had finally caught up with her.

"I know, Kim. It's got to be finished. But if we fight, more men will die. It's wrong, it's all wrong."

"You said something about when the country grows up, men like me will disappear. I don't think so, Rocky. There'll always be things like this."

"Not if the law is strong," she whispered. "This wouldn't have happened if Ed Lane was a different man than he is."

Kim nodded, knowing it was true. He had seen this played out time after time. Different names, different scenes, but essentially the same grim drama of strength bullying weakness. When law was only an ideal, a theory, people like Hank Dunning and Peg Cody, consumed by greed and ambition, could not be controlled, but the right kind of man wearing the star could make law something more than a theory.

The fault went back to the complacency of the

people who permitted Lane's election. Brit Bonham and Doc Frazee as well as Fred Galt. And Kim Logan. He had not been here when Lane had been elected, but he had been in other places where the same thing had been done, and he had stood by, doing nothing.

"We'll get a different man," he said. "Now you'd better get some rest. You can't do anything for Shorty by standing here. It's out of your hands."

"Out of my hands," she breathed. "Yes, I guess it is."

She left the room, Kim following. Rocky went on into the kitchen. Doc Frazee had laid his black bag on the pine table in the middle of the front room and had dropped into a rocking chair. Kim drew another chair up beside him and sat down.

"How bad is he, Doc?" he asked.

"Pretty bad," Frazee said gloomily. "Busted ribs. Concussion. A face that'll never look the same again." He shook his head. "They must have knocked him down and booted the tar out of him. Pretty brave outfit, that bunch." Frazee gave him a straight look. "What are you going to do?"

"Why should I do anything?" Kim motioned toward the kitchen. Talk flowed through the open door, Mrs. Fawcett's voice rising above the girls', her tone bitter and accusing. "Della's ma don't believe I will."

Frazee stroked his goatee, his bony face grave. "I'll tell you," he said finally. "Some of us have our bets down on you . . . me and Brit and Rocky. Della, too, or she wouldn't have brought you out here. You goin' to welsh on them bets?"

"I didn't make the bets," Kim said.

"Well, we made 'em for you. It adds up to the same thing."

"Looks to me like a thankless job. About like pulling a drowning man out of the river. He'll fight you while you're saving him."

"Yeah, I know," Frazee said gloomily. "Same thing with me. Cuss me because I dose 'em with medicine that don't taste good, but I keep on dosing 'em. Don't ask me why. I just do it."

Della came out of the kitchen. "Breakfast is ready," she said.

They ate by lamplight, Mrs. Fawcett plodding between the table and the big range to fill coffee cups or bring more biscuits and bacon. When they were done, a faint gray light had crept across the eastern sky.

"Time to ride, Kim," Della said. "I'm going with you, but Rocky's staying with her pa."

Kim rose, nodding. Mrs. Fawcett stood with her back to the stove, a wide-hipped, shapeless woman, the mark of the hard years on her face and hands, on a body that might once have been as slim and attractive as her daughter's.

"Don't you get into none of the fighting, Della," Mrs. Fawcett said. "You come back here when the palaver's finished." Then she looked directly at Kim, doubt clouding her broad face. "We'll see how much smell a skunk can make, mister, and maybe you'll find out what a bunch of sheep can do."

"Then Hank Dunning and Dutch Heinz will be surprised," Kim said.

For just a moment Kim stood looking at Rocky, filling his eyes with the vibrant young beauty of her face. Then he wheeled and followed Della out of the house.

It was full daylight when Kim and Della reached the clearing where only a few hours before the Avis buildings had stood. Now there was nothing but the piles of gray ashes where the cabin and barn and other buildings had been. The cabin's chimney was still standing, a grim monument that would be here long after the ashes were scattered.

Kim had not wanted Della to come with him, but he knew that, if he went alone, he would never convince the mesa ranchers of his honest intentions. Now, riding across the clearing, he saw that Della's presence was even more necessary than he had first thought.

Six men were hunkered in the yard, idly talking and smoking. The instant Kim was recognized, they stood up, hands dropping to gun butts. They began backing toward their horses, wary eyes on Kim. They would have started shooting before he had ridden half the width of the clearing if Della had not been with him.

Della and Kim reined up ten paces from the men, Della smiling as if this was a pleasant social gathering. She motioned toward Kim.

"Boys, you know Kim Logan, don't you?" she said.

"I'm sorry I do," one of them said. "What the devil you doing here, Logan?"

"I'm throwing in with you," Kim said. "You could use another gun."

They scowled, finding his words mentally indigestible. He dismounted, gave Della a hand, and swung away from the group. There would be enough explaining to do when the rest got here. He made a wide circle around the yard, leaving Della to talk to her neighbors. Presently two others rode in, and after ten minutes had passed Abe Fawcett arrived with a rancher named Clay Mackey. That was all. Kim joined the group then, standing beside Della and facing the others.

There was no talk for a time. Della had apparently said all that she could, and it hadn't been enough. They eyed him a moment, anger stirring in them.

"I've always had quite a bit of faith in Della's judgment in things like this, Logan," Fawcett said then, "but I'm blamed if I do this time. She says you want to throw in with us. Why?"

Kim stood motionlessly, his back held stiffly straight, his probing blue eyes making a cool study of these men. Fawcett was as near a leader as there was among them. Big-chested and paunchy, Abe Fawcett had steel-gray eyes and silver hair that gave him a sort of dignity, but his appearance would have been more impressive if he had not worn a sweeping mustache that added a faintly comical touch to a face that otherwise was severe.

Most of these men were, like Fawcett and Shorty Avis, middle-aged or older. Only two were young, sons who had stayed with their fathers. Most of the boys had drifted out of the country, knowing they weren't needed at home and that there was little chance of finding work in Ganado. The only possible jobs were with the HD and the Clawhammer. None of them wanted those jobs except Clay Mackey's three boys who were riding for the Clawhammer.

"Well?" Fawcett prodded.

"I'll tell you why," Kim said, bringing his eyes to the big man. "We're on the same side. I can use some help and you can use another gun, so we'd be smart to team up."

Little Joe Scanlon at the end of the line shook his head. "It wouldn't be smart, mister. It'd be plain stupid. You've been riding around talking tough for the Clawhammer. Been a year now. We've got no reason to think you've changed." He motioned around the clearing. "It's my guess you had a hand in this."

"You're guessing wrong, Joe," Kim said mildly.

"A lot's happened in the last three or four days. Everything's turned inside out. No use taking time to tell all of it, but there's two things you need to know. I couldn't have been here because Ed Lane had me in the jug for a killing that Phil Martin and Hank Dunning rigged. After I got out, I was too busy keeping my neck out of a rope to be in on a torch party. The second thing is that Peg Cody fired me."

They were silent a moment, weighing his words in their minds.

"I ain't satisfied," Fawcett said. "You could pull us into a trap and get our heads shot off. We know you'd been warned to stay off Shorty's property." He motioned toward the chimney. "Might be your way of getting square with Shorty."

Kim shoved his thumbs into his belt, eyes moving along the line of hostile faces. "I'll tell you something else which I hadn't aimed to, but it's what makes the difference in me. I love Rocky."

They might have cursed him for wanting one of their women. Or laughed at him. They did neither. Instead they shifted uneasily, toes digging into the dirt, and he saw at once that he had said the one right thing.

"You fixing to marry her and live up here?" Clay Mackey demanded.

"I haven't asked her," Kim answered, "but I will if I'm alive when this is settled. If I live and

251

Rocky will have me, we'll stay in the valley, but not here on the mesa. I don't think you boys will, either. You'll be back on the creek where you belong."

Fawcett blew out a great breath, fat jowls trembling. "What kind of a fairy tale are you getting off?"

Kim smiled. "No fairy tale, Abe. Let me ask you a question. Why did you round these boys up?"

"Huh? You can see for yourself. I had a look at Shorty when Rocky fetched him in. I . . . why, damn it, Logan, I wanted the boys to see what the Clawhammer will do if we don't stop 'em."

"How do you aim to stop the Clawhammer?"

"Well, I . . . I thought we'd figure out something this morning."

XVIII

Once more Kim swung his gaze along the line of faces, not so hostile now, faces weathered by wind and sun, faces of men who wanted nothing but the right to live in peace, and deeply frightened because they knew there was no peace for them.

"Then you need me," Kim said to Fawcett. "I know what to do."

Again the men shifted uneasily, wanting his help but still uncertain about him.

252

"Don't stand there like a bunch of ninnies," Della said. "Tell him we'll work with him."

"We could use some help," Fawcett said reluctantly, "but even if you're on the level, Logan, your gun won't make the difference. Dunning's outfit is at the Clawhammer. We just ain't tough enough to lick 'em."

"So you'll run again like you ran once before when Sam Cody kicked you off the creek," Kim said with biting contempt. "You don't think you can win if you hang and rattle. You're wrong, Abe. I say you can."

"I reckon we'll go along with you," Joe Scanlon said. "Trouble is we allowed you'd be the one who did Peg Cody's pushing."

"Not me," Kim said. "I figured she was scrapping with Dunning, but it don't look that way now. Anyhow, it's Dunning and Dutch Heinz who'll do the pushing, and they can be licked."

Kim hunkered in the dirt and, picking up a stick, sketched a map of the valley.

"My notion is to divide the valley. If others come in, we'll make room for 'em. This can be a good cattle country for all of us. A lot of folks can make a living here without fighting and without making hogs out of themselves."

He drew several lines across his map.

"I ain't trying to tell you how to divide the valley, but it might work like this. Fawcett here." He made an F. "Scanlon here." He went on down the line, following the east side of the creek, filling in initials. "It means buying good bulls and more cows. Putting up buildings and corrals. Going off and leaving what you've done here." He rose, facing them. "Remember one thing. If you'd fought Sam Cody a long time ago, you wouldn't be up here." He pointed at his map. "You'd be down there."

"This is worse than a fairy tale!" Fawcett burst out. "We're trying to think of some way to save our homes, not move back to the creek and give Peg Cody a real excuse to wipe us out."

"You mean you wouldn't go back to the creek, Abe?" Kim asked. "They tell me you used to be quite a cowman."

Fawcett got red in the face; his fat jowls were trembling again. He tried to say something and failed.

"Even if we did move in on the Clawhammer and made it stick," Joe Scanlon said, "this would take money. We couldn't swing it, Logan."

"Brit Bonham's got money to loan," Kim said. "I talked to him about it yesterday. I claim that a lot of little outfits will bring more prosperity to this country than two big ones. Brit will gamble, if you boys will gamble your lives."

"We've got till sunset," Clay Mackey said worriedly.

"Maybe not that long. I'm guessing, but I figure Peg will leave her crew with the herd. It's

Dunning's bunch we'll have to fight." Kim pinned his eyes on Mackey. "If Peg was pulling her crew in, your boys would have been home before this, wouldn't they?"

"That's right," Mackey said, "if they knew what was up."

"I know the way Peg thinks," Kim went on. "It'll be cattle first and fight second. We lick Dunning and our troubles are over."

"Not if we're moving back on the creek." Scanlon pointed at the map. "That's Clawhammer range you're giving away."

"The Clawhammer's done," Kim said. "Peg don't know it, but that's the way it is, providing we finish Dunning. The bank will close Peg out."

Fawcett shook his head doubtfully. "Bonham won't close her out."

"He will. You'll see."

Fawcett swung to face his neighbors. "I wanted you boys to see this. Maybe it's Dunning or maybe it's the Clawhammer, or both. Whichever way it is, you see what you're up against. Now we'd best get home. We'll keep our eyes open and . . ."

"No," Kim said.

Fawcett wheeled to face him. "You ain't giving the orders."

"I am if I'm with you in this ruckus."

"He said he knew what to do," Scanlon said.

"All right," Fawcett muttered reluctantly. "If you've got a plan, let's hear it."

"Fighting's an old game to me," Kim said, "but a blind man could see it's new to you. If you go back to your homes, you're licked. Dunning will finish you one at a time. The only chance you've got is to stick together and take the fight to them. If you want your women safe, let Della fetch 'em to her place."

"There wouldn't be nobody there to fight . . . ," Fawcett began.

"I've got a hunch your women will put up quite a scrap. Now I'll tell you what I want you to do. Give me half an hour's start. Then you light out for the Clawhammer, but don't go on down. Leave your horses on the bench, back where they won't be seen from the house. Then wait there. About noon or after Dunning and his boys will ride out. Let 'em get close before you give it to 'em. Surprise has won more fights than hot lead, and they'll sure be surprised."

"We'll be leaving our homes wide open," Scanlon objected.

"They'll be wide open if you all go home and figure on fighting by yourselves. Dunning will figure on you running again."

They looked at each other, bitter men, shamed by their past record, held here now only by their pride. Watching them, Kim could not be sure what the end would be. Welding them into a fighting unit was about as difficult as making a ball of dry sand.

"All right," Clay Mackey said at last. "We'll be there."

"Where are you going?" Fawcett demanded.

"To the Clawhammer."

"You can't, Kim!" Della cried. "They'll kill you."

"Maybe," Kim agreed, "but I'm figuring on surprise being on my side. Anyhow, there's a thing or two I need to know."

"And something they'll need to know!" Scanlon shouted. "You can tell 'em where we'll be."

"I could." Kim turned to his buckskin and stepped up. He sat his saddle, eyes searching their faces. "I may need some help if it don't go like I figure."

"If Rocky was here, she wouldn't let you do this," Della said.

Leaning down, he said in a low tone: "I've never told Rocky I love her. If I don't see her again, I'd like for her to know."

Reining his horse around, he rode across the clearing and into the timber.

It was well toward noon when Kim reached the bench above the Clawhammer and looked down on the big house and barns and maze of corrals. Sam Cody had built well, certain of his future and equally certain that he had trained Peg to run the ranch as efficiently as he had. But there are always two uncertain factors over which a cowman has little control—weather and the price of beef. They had beaten bigger men than Sam Cody, and they had beaten him. Peg had inherited Sam Cody's ambition and lax ethics, so she was using the same ruthless, pushing tactics he had used.

Kim, sitting his saddle, found the same questions prodding his mind that had been there for hours. How much had Peg ever really counted on him? Had she turned fully to Dutch Heinz? Had she gone to Dunning or had Dunning come to her? That was the difference between her and her father. She was forced to look to men to help carry out her plans; Sam had needed no one. Still, the answers to these questions were not important, not when Kim thought of Yuma Bill, of Shorty Avis, and the ashes that had been Rocky's home. Kim would kill Hank Dunning as quickly as he would kill any wild animal that needed killing. He would do the same to Dutch Heinz. But he could not beat Peg down with his fists; he could not draw a gun on her. Even the law would not touch her unless the evidence against her was conclusive.

Kim rode down off the bench and crossed the creek. He could not make a definite plan of action until he saw the shape of things. There were those who would have said he was crazy for coming in like this, but it seemed worth the risk. Regardless of the part Peg had in the trouble,

Hank Dunning was the hub around which it revolved. With Dunning dead, trouble would disintegrate like a whirling wheel coming apart, and a dozen lives would be saved. It was a gamble, Kim Logan's life balanced against those that might be saved.

There was a knot of men in front of the barn. Dunning's riders, Kim saw as he came up, but Dunning was not with them. They were covertly watching Kim while appearing to be idling. Limpy was not in sight. Neither was Dutch Heinz.

It was as peaceful a scene as a man would find, too peaceful, and Kim was warned by the very innocence of it. He reined up and dismounted, keeping the buckskin between him and the men by the barn. While he tied, his eyes swept the yard. Apparently no one else was around. He stepped away from the hitch pole and deliberately rolled a smoke, standing so that Dunning's men could see him.

The thing was so casual that it must have been carefully planned to appear this way. Kim felt a chill down his spine as he considered the two things he could do. He could walk straight toward Dunning's crew with his gun in his hand, or he could ignore them and go into the house. Dunning was probably inside, and because Dunning was the man he wanted, he chose the house. It was too late to back out now. He had to play it through.

He fired his cigarette and flipped the match

away, then turned up the path to the house. The front door was open. No one was in sight in the big living room. He stepped up on the porch, throwing a quick glance at the men in front of the barn. They were tense now. He went on across the porch, hand on gun butt. If he read the sign right, this was trouble.

Kim stepped through the door. He had no chance to pull his gun. Dutch Heinz was waiting for him, back pressed against the wall. He slammed into Kim, big fist battering him in the stomach. It was treacherous and unexpected, a brutal blow that slammed wind out of him and sent him reeling back through the door. He had a brief glimpse of Peg and Dunning behind Heinz. He heard a yell from the men at the barn and the pound of boots as they ran toward the house.

Heinz had a slow, stubborn mind, the sort that never forgave. Now the need to square accounts with Kim made a maniac out of him. He hammered Kim in the stomach, on the chest, on the head. Kim had been caught off balance and kept that way; he had no chance to swing an effective fist. He backed across the porch, trying to block Heinz's blows, but it was like trying to dam a stream in high flood.

Kim fell off the porch. He landed on his back and yanked his gun clear of leather. Heinz was poised on the edge of the porch to jump on him, but he held himself there, teetering and swearing.

Kim lay motionless, gun tilted up to cover Heinz, while he fought to drag breath into aching lungs.

Dunning's men were there then, but they didn't close in, for the first move would have brought death to Heinz. Slowly Kim came to his feet.

"You've got an iron, Dutch," he said. "I'm putting mine back. Then we'll settle this."

Heinz shook his head. "Not me. I heard about Tonto Miles." He motioned to Dunning's men. "You're done, Logan. Too many of us. What'n hell did you ride in here for?"

"I didn't expect this." Kim backed away now so that he could watch Heinz and Dunning's crew. "I thought you'd be out of the country. Ed Lane's looking for you."

Heinz laughed jeeringly. "Not now he ain't. He was out here this morning, but he decided he didn't want to be sheriff no more. He's halfway to Del Norte by now. We don't have no sheriff at all now, not any."

Dunning had crossed the porch to stand beside Heinz, towering above him, his black hair rebellious and uncombed. A smile touched the corners of his long-lipped mouth; his dark eyes seemed entirely lacking in expression. Somehow Dunning was able to clothe himself with a sort of arrogant dignity. It was that dignity that had given him the reputation he had in the valley.

"Why are you here, Logan?" Dunning asked.

"Natural enough for me to be here," Kim

answered. "But it ain't for you. Or maybe you're taking over the Clawhammer."

Dunning shrugged. "Maybe I am. Or the Clawhammer's taking over the HD. I want to know why you're here."

"I want to see Peg."

Dunning jerked his head at the door. "Put your gun up. She's inside."

"I'll keep my gun in my fist. I'm not giving my back to your wolf pack."

"Drop your gun, Kim!" Peg called. "You'll have a chance to see me, but not with a gun in your hand."

She was behind him. She must have come around the house. He made a slow turn, saw the Winchester in her hand. He had no doubt she would use it, for she was close now to what she had been working for.

"Looks like your pot," Kim said, and shoved his gun into holster.

Heinz came off the porch in a headlong rush. Kim sidestepped and swung a fist to Heinz's face as he charged by. Then the roof fell on Kim. Dunning's crew swarmed over him and he went down. He struck out, squirmed and kicked, tried to roll, to break free, but there were too many. They smothered him by sheer weight, but even then, with consciousness almost battered out of him, he heard Peg's voice.

"Quit it! I said it was enough!"

Kim lay on his back, winded and hurt, staring up

at men who seemed to be ten feet tall. Peg was standing over Kim, her cocked Winchester held on the ready.

"Hank," she said, "maybe it was a good thing this happened. Now get this through your head. Marrying me won't make any difference about one thing. I'm giving the orders here and keep on giving them."

"You're forgetting Chuck Dale," Dunning said in a low bitter voice. "The boy I lost off the rim the day Logan brought Yuma Bill here. You're forgetting Tonto Miles and Pat Monroney. And you're forgetting you said Logan was just a drifter you could get rid of any time you wanted to. He's blocked everything we've tried from the minute he took Yuma Bill off the stage, and I aim to stop it."

"I'm not going to stand here and let your boys kick Kim to death," Peg snapped. "Not after I told him he'd have a chance to see me."

"He's been plenty hard to kill," Dunning said in the same bitter tone. "We'd best do the job while we've got his fangs pulled."

"He'll wait," Peg said. "Your boys have got a job to do. Get them started on it."

"Not time yet," Dunning said.

For a moment they stood facing each other, straight-backed and proud, their wills clashing. Then Dunning broke under the force of Peg's stare and motioned his men back to the barn.

Heinz remained by the steps, great shoulders hunched forward in characteristic ape-like posture.

"You've made some mistakes before, Peg," he said, "but saving this *hombre*'s hide is the biggest one. You're soft."

"Soft?" Peg shook her head. "I just think a little further than you do, Dutch. Kim may be some good to us alive, but he's no good to anybody dead." She prodded Kim with a toe. "Get up. I'm locking you in the storeroom."

Kim got to his feet, reeling a little as he wiped a sleeve across his battered face. Peg pulled his gun. He stood staring at her. Her red hair was carelessly pinned on her head, and her hazel eyes that he had so often seen filled with good humor were sharp and calculating.

Kim walked past the glowering Heinz and into the house. He went on through the kitchen and into the storeroom behind it, stumbling, for he was still groggy from the beating he had taken. He dropped down on a sack of sugar and held his head, a steady pain flashing across his temples.

Peg stood in the doorway, looking at him.

"I wish you hadn't come here, Kim," she said. "I wish you hadn't."

She closed the door, twisted the turn pin. There had been a note of sincere regret in her voice as if she had been talking to a man condemned to death.

XIX

Logan had never been one to doubt his own destiny, but there were doubts in his mind now. He was in a tighter spot than when Ed Lane had locked him up in the Ganado jail. He'd had a few friends in town, but here he had none.

He walked around the room that was filled with the Clawhammer's supplies. Sam Cody must have planned it for a jail. There were only two windows, both high and so small that a grown man could not have escaped through either of them. The door was at the other end of the room. Kim had often wondered why a storeroom needed a door so thick and so solidly hinged.

Kim put a shoulder against the door and pushed. There was no give to it. He stepped away and slammed against it and bounced back. No use. Kim had no illusions about his position. It was practically hopeless. He didn't know why Peg had saved his life. Sooner or later Dunning and Heinz would wear her down, and they'd have their way with him.

It must have been close to an hour after Kim had been locked in the storeroom that the door swung open. Limpy came in with a plate of food and a steaming cup of coffee. Peg stood behind him with her Winchester.

"I'm going to town this afternoon," she said, "and I didn't want you to get hungry."

Limpy set the plate and cup down on a box.

"You sure played the devil coming back, Logan," he said. "Why didn't you have sense enough to stay away?"

"I didn't figure Peg meant it when she said I was fired," Kim answered.

Peg waited until Limpy left the storeroom.

"Don't try to jump me," she said. "Hank and Dutch want you dead. I don't."

"Maybe you mean you don't want the job of beefing me. You can always hire somebody to do dirty jobs like that."

Two spots of red showed on her cheeks, but she held her temper.

"No, I mean I don't want you killed, but I don't know what to do with you. I've done some things I'm ashamed of because I've been a little crazy with my dreams about the Clawhammer, but I haven't knowingly been guilty of killing. Please believe that."

"Maybe you think Yuma Bill died of measles."

"No. Dutch shot him, but not because I ordered it. I told him to take the money, but like a fool he didn't wear a mask, so he killed the old man to shut his mouth." Peg was silent while she watched Kim. Then she asked: "Why did you really come here?"

"To get Dunning. That's what you hired me for."

"What made you think you'd find him here?"

"Rocky said you and him were working together. She says you're in love with him."

"The Clawhammer's the only thing I love!" she flared. "You ought to know that by now."

"So you're marrying Dunning because you love the Clawhammer. Now that makes a lot of sense."

"Of course it does. After I marry Hank, there won't be any HD. Just Clawhammer range on both sides of the creek."

"Think you can run Dunning?"

"I never saw a man I couldn't run. Except you." She shook her head. "Kim, I'm sorry the way it's gone between us, but I gave you every chance and you wouldn't take it."

"You'd already promised Dunning, hadn't you?"

She shrugged. "A promise doesn't mean much to me. I aimed to buy the best husband I could get. I thought for a while you'd be the one, but I found out you had too many fool notions about the mesa ranchers."

"The Clawhammer's got along without the mesa range."

"It won't. Not with the plans I have. Anyhow, you're too soft. Or maybe it was because you're in love with Rocky Avis. Anyhow, I found out you wouldn't do."

"No, I reckon I wouldn't. Looks to me like you've got some pretty big schemes cooked up for the Clawhammer, or you wouldn't want the mesa range so bad."

She nodded with satisfaction. "I have. And I won't grow old waiting to do what I want to do. The Clawhammer will be the biggest outfit in the state. Maybe in the nation. I'll have the valley and the mesa and the high range to boot. All mine, just like I told you that night."

"The little fry won't run, Peg. You've fixed it so you've got to win or you're finished."

She laughed scornfully. "I will win, and you're loco about the little fry. They'll run all right. Dad's mistake was in not chasing them across the Divide."

"You're wrong, Peg. Why can't you hang onto what you've got and be satisfied?"

"I wasn't born to be satisfied. I don't have the slightest doubt about the way this will go. When a man has run once, he'll run again. That's why I'm going to town this afternoon. They'll be there to sell to me."

"You gave the order to bust Shorty Avis up?"

She nodded. "I had to show them what would happen if they had any notion of fighting. Before I'm done, I'll have the little fry off the other side of the valley, too."

Kim finished his meal, thinking he had heard the truth from Peg at last. She was a greedy fool, reaching for everything when most people would have been satisfied with what she had. She had been carried away by the magnificence of her dreams, was counting on Hank Dunning and Dutch Heinz, and in the end she would destroy herself.

"Funny thing," he said. "I guess I know you better than anyone in the valley."

She laughed lightly. "Of course you do. I still wish you were on my side, but it's too late now." Her face turned grave then. "You insist on being a man, Kim, and that's the reason I knew I couldn't manage you." She motioned toward the rear wall. "Step back and I'll get your plate and cup. I've got to ride."

He moved back.

"Why did you hire me and put out this fake war talk?" he asked.

"Money. I wanted a lot of money to stock Clawhammer range, so I borrowed thirty thousand from Bonham. I got his sympathy by telling him Dunning would push me off the range if I didn't hold it. Of course, I didn't want him or anyone else to know that Dunning was going to work up a run on his bank so we could buy my notes back. It would have worked if you hadn't delivered Yuma Bill's money."

Peg picked up Kim's plate and cup and moved back to the door, smiling ruefully.

"As for hiring you, I had to make some show of protecting myself against Hank. You rode in just when I was looking for a tough hand and you looked like one." She stood there, looking at him, frowning. "Maybe I'll figure out what to do with you while I'm gone. I just wish you'd ridden off like I told you to."

She moved out of the storeroom, her Winchester covering him until the door swung shut. It was clear enough now. Bonham had fallen into Peg's trap when he'd loaned her the $30,000, and the fake war had accomplished exactly what Peg had wanted it to. She was pretending to hold out against a ruthless neighbor, and, because she was a woman, she had succeeded in winning sympathy. In her way she was a genius, hiding her real ambition from Brit Bonham and Doc Frazee and the rest of the townsmen. $30,000 for $10,000! That was how her deal with Bonham had been meant to work. Dunning had been in Bonham's office that morning trying to buy Peg's notes and Bonham had come close to making the deal. Kim laughed, a sour laugh, for it was a sour kind of joke, this sympathy they'd had for Peg while she had been planning a neat profit of $20,000.

It hadn't worked, but still Peg was talking about having the biggest outfit in the state or even in the nation. Wild talk, the crazy talk of a woman consumed by ambition. Crazy or not, she was coldly logical. She had another idea to make quick money, a lot of money, for her grandiose plans would not include any penny ante business.

A sense of futility touched Kim. This thing still

had to be fought to its irrevocable end. Dunning and Dutch Heinz had to die, and Peg would have to leave the valley, but here he was, a prisoner. The chances were good that while Peg was gone, Heinz would come in and shoot him.

Kim realized now that for all of Peg's expressed love for the Clawhammer and her wild dreams, there was a real difference between her and Dutch Heinz and Dunning. She had a soft spot whether she would admit it or not; Heinz and Dunning did not. She had saved his life today. By that one act she showed that the gulf between her and these men she thought she was using was wide and deep.

There was no sense in sitting here and waiting for Heinz to come in and finish him. Kim began searching the room for some kind of a weapon, any kind that would give him a chance. There was nothing. Not even an axe handle. In desperation, he kicked a flour barrel apart, coughing as a white cloud swirled up around his head. He picked up a stave, balanced it in his hand, and shook his head. A sorry weapon, but the best he could find.

He walked to the door, shoved some boxes out of the corner, and moved into it, putting his back against the wall. Somebody would come after him, probably Heinz, and, if he didn't see him, it would be natural enough to step inside. The barrel stave, brought down in a sharp blow across a man's wrist, would make him drop a gun. Then Kim would have a chance, for there would be a moment of shocked, painful surprise that would give Kim an opportunity to beat him to the dropped gun.

The big house must have been deserted, for no sound came as the minutes dragged by. Then another hope came to Kim. Perhaps Dunning and Heinz had ridden out. They might not return until after Peg did. Still, although she had saved his life once, it was doubtful if she could do it again.

Suddenly Kim was aware of gunfire. He ran to a window and looked out, but he could not see anyone. The shooting came from the north, and he could see nothing but the bench directly behind the house. Anxiety growing in him, he guessed what had happened. The mesa ranchers had waited on the other side of the creek, and, when Dunning and his bunch had left the Clawhammer, they'd ridden into an unexpected fight.

The firing grew closer. Then Kim heard steps on the kitchen floor. He drew back into his corner, raising the stave. The door was pulled open.

"Logan . . . Logan!" Limpy called. "Where are you?"

Kim's hands tightened on the stave, but Limpy did not come in.

"Logan, here's your gun!" he cried again, his voice frantic. "No sense hiding this way. I don't like Dunning's bunch no better than you do."

Kim didn't understand, but this was no time to wonder why Limpy was doing this. The shooting was almost in front of the house now. Kim lunged through the door, knocking the gun out of Limpy's hand.

"What'd you do that for?" the old man yelled. "I was just trying to help. . . ."

Kim scooped up the gun. "I didn't know whether you were alone or not."

"Nobody else around here who'd give you a hand!" Limpy cried. "I can see that horse thief of a Dunning if Peg can't. I kept telling her she had no business letting him come around here. She can't make no silk purse out of a sow's ear. She should have taken a shotgun to Dunning the first time. . . ."

But Kim wasn't waiting to hear the old man. He checked the gun, ran out of the kitchen, through the living room, and onto the porch. The fight was directly in front of the house. It was the last thing Kim expected. The mesa ranchers had got the jump on Dunning's riders and had chased them back across the creek.

The yard was filled with milling horses, smoke made a swirling fog over them, guns roared, and men shouted and bawled wild oaths and cried shrilly in agony. Kim stepped down off the porch, thinking that this would be the end, one way or the other, that it could be fought out to a final bloody finish here in the Clawhammer's yard.

Dutch Heinz bawled out an order above the uproar: "Inside! Inside!"

Heinz came off his horse and plunged toward the house, some of Dunning's crew following.

Then Heinz saw Kim and he stopped, flat-footed, with a strangled involuntary cry. Kim sensed the fear that was in the man in this one quick look at the wide-jawed face. Heinz had his gun in his hand. He came on, lifting his .45 and throwing a shot at Kim—too late, for Kim had laced a bullet into his great chest.

Heinz rocked forward and fell, hands flung out, and lay still. Kim stepped over him and went on. He felt the sting of a slug gouging flesh away from a rib. He fired again and knocked another man off his feet. Limpy, on the porch behind Kim, let go with a shotgun, the load of buckshot blowing a huge hole in a man's stomach.

It was enough. Caught between Kim's and Limpy's fire on one side and that of the mesa ranchers on the other, the rest of Dunning's outfit threw up their hands. "Hold it!" Kim called. "Hold it!"

There were four of them still on their feet, two wounded, and two untouched by bullets but badly scared and having all desire for fighting knocked out of them. Kim kept them covered until Abe Fawcett tramped up, his neighbors strung out behind him, some bleeding from bullet wounds, but all filled with the glow of complete and unexpected victory.

"Where's Dunning?" Kim demanded.

Fawcett stopped, surprised, as if he had not thought of Dunning, and stared at the dead men on the ground.

"Why, I never saw Dunning," he said. "Maybe he wasn't with 'em."

"He wasn't," Joe Scanlon said. "Heinz was running the outfit. They rode right into us. Didn't figure we were within ten miles of here. It was like you said, Logan. Surprise was worth a couple of cannons. We knocked the devil out of 'em with the first volley. They lit out for here and we got on their tails as soon as we could hit leather."

Kim motioned to Fawcett. "Take these *hombres* inside. Patch 'em. Looks like some of your boys need a little patching, too." He swung to face Limpy. "Where's Dunning?"

Limpy threw a scared look at the mesa men. "Kim, you tell these *hombres* I helped you. Tell 'em I didn't like Dunning and Heinz, neither."

"All right, all right," Kim said hurriedly. "Hear that, Abe? Limpy's on our side. Treat him right."

"You bet," Fawcett said. "I seen what he done with that scatter-gun."

"Where's Dunning?" Kim asked again.

But Limpy was not to be hurried. "What about Peg? This ain't her fault. It was Dunning's and Heinz's."

"I want to know where Dunning is!" Kim shouted in exasperation. "What's the matter with you?"

Limpy gripped his shotgun with white-knuckled hands, harried eyes swinging around the half circle of men in front of him.

"He's in town. Rode in with Peg. I want to know about her. I promised Sam the day he died that I'd look out for her. I tried to keep her out of this, but she was too stubborn to listen. You can't hang a woman. What about her, Kim?"

"She's got to leave the valley," Kim said. "If she don't try to make more trouble, she won't be hurt. That's the only promise I can make."

Limpy licked dry lips, trembling now as he pinned his gaze on Kim. "Dunning aimed to show up in town and tell folks that him and Peg had buried the hatchet. No more trouble. Then about dusk he was goin' to leave. These fellers was supposed to run everybody off the mesa this afternoon and they'd swear Dunning was with 'em all night. Then after dark he was going back to town to rob the bank. He was goin' to take all the cash and get Peg's notes."

Then it wasn't over. It wouldn't be over until Hank Dunning was dead. Kim put a hand to his side where the bullet had raked a rib. He drew his hand away and stared blankly at the blood, trying to think what was to be done.

"Let's go get Dunning and hang him!" Scanlon shouted.

"I'll get him," Kim said. "I'll send Doc out. Take care of your wounded. I'll fetch Heinz's body with me so Dunning will see how it is. You can bring the rest in later."

"You'll need help," Scanlon said.

Kim shook his head. "No. This is my job. I'll do it. Alone."

XX

It was late afternoon when Kim reached the fringe of cabins that surrounded Ganado. He was leading Heinz's horse, the dead man lashed face down across the saddle. All the way in he had thought about Peg. She had saved his life. He would probably never know exactly what her motive had been, but the fact that she had saved his life could not be questioned. Whatever she had done and planned to do, he owed a debt to her.

Before Kim had left the Clawhammer, Limpy had drawn him aside. "Peg just couldn't look ahead," the old man had said. "She ain't bad. She was just mixed up about what she could make men do. Dunning wanted to marry her, but then there would have been no Clawhammer. Just the HD. Heinz knew that, but Dunning was paying him, unbeknownst to Peg. All them shenanigans like busting Bonham and getting Peg's notes cheap was Dunning's ideas. If Sam had lived, he'd have busted Dunning sooner or later, but after Sam cashed in, Dunning set to work on Peg, telling her how they'd have the biggest outfit in the valley, chase the little fellers out, and put more cows on this range than there is in the state of Texas. She took it all in, bait, hook, and sinker." Limpy had gripped Kim's arm then. "I tell you she ain't bad, boy! Young and foolish and full of big wild ideas. That's all. She just didn't see all the misery she was bringing on the valley. Take care of her, will you?"

There had been nothing for Kim to say except to repeat: "She'll have to leave the valley. She won't be hurt if she does."

"Then I'll go with her," Limpy had said. "Tell her that."

Now, with Ganado before him, Kim did not know what to say to Peg. His thoughts were on her rather than on Dunning, for there was no doubt of Dunning's part in this trouble but there was of Peg's. She was stubborn and she was proud, and she would not easily give up the fine dreams that had been hers. She had told him of dreaming about what she was going to do and thinking of the mistakes her father had made. She wouldn't make them; she would use the weapons given a woman. It struck Kim that it was Sam Cody who was really to blame for what Peg had done. He had died, plagued by a sense of failure, and Peg had been driven by an obsession to carry those plans to fulfillment.

Kim rode down Main Street, watching for

Dunning and Peg, and seeing neither of them. He reined up and dismounted. Someone saw him and raised a cry. Men crowded around him—Bonham and Doc Frazee and Johnny Naylor and half a dozen more—all throwing questions at him.

Kim handed Bonham a heavy money belt. "I reckon that's Yuma Bill's. I took it off Heinz."

He told them what had happened. He stopped talking suddenly as Bonham said softly: "There's Dunning."

Dunning stood in front of the hotel, bare-headed, his hair freshly trimmed and slicked down. Peg was in the lobby, staring through a window, and Kim could not see the expression on her face. But there was no mistaking Dunning's. The HD owner must have been surprised to see Kim; he must have been more surprised when he saw Heinz's body. But there was more than surprise on his eagle-beaked face. There was a cold and bitter hatred for this man he had regarded too lightly. His lips were pulled so tightly against his teeth that they made a thin bitter line. He still wore his cloak of arrogant dignity, but the cool assurance that was usually a part of him was gone.

Kim stood motionlessly a few feet in front of the horse that carried Heinz's body, the slanting sunlight hard upon him, his shadow a long dark streak at his side. He was remembering Tonto Miles and his own thoughts when he had fought

Miles. He had been forced to kill the man to get at Dunning. Now the moment was here.

The seconds ticked by. The town was quiet, waiting. Still Dunning stood there, his face mirroring the cold rage that gripped him. Then Kim spoke.

"Your string's wound up, Dunning. The mesa bunch was waiting for your outfit and shot 'em to rags."

Dunning's hand was within inches of gun butt, his black eyes on Kim as he took two deliberate steps. That was all. Then his hand moved toward gun butt, fast, and the barrel was clear of leather and coming up.

Two shots rolled out together, the reports, hammering against the false front of Ganado's Main Street, were thrown back, and faded. Two shots, no more. Kim stood motionlessly, smoke curling up from the muzzle of his .44, and waited until Dunning's knees gave and he spilled forward and the slanting sunlight fell across his back.

Someone yelled from the front of the drug store, a high yell that was almost a scream. Another gun sounded from the boardwalk behind Kim and to his right. He whirled, his .44 coming up. Then he lowered it. It was Johnny Naylor who had fired. He held his Colt in front of him, eyes fixed on the drug store. Kim turning to look, saw Phil Martin clad only in his underwear, fall forward out of the doorway. Then Kim knew what had happened.

Martin, dog-like in his devotion, had made this futile effort to square accounts for Hank Dunning.

"Thanks, Johnny," Kim said. "I didn't expect that from you."

Naylor gave him a tight grin. "Della's been currying me with her tongue ever since the stage got in. You're right, Logan. She pounded that into me."

Kim slipped his gun into holster and walked across the street to the hotel. He stepped into the lobby. Peg stood motionlessly at the window. She said without turning: "Looks like I put my money on the wrong man."

"The wrong man," he said, and walked to her. "Now you're finished."

"You haven't touched the Clawhammer," she said.

"Bonham will do that. The biggest mistake you made was to think that because a man ran once he'd run again." He told her what had happened at the Clawhammer, and added: "You've got one chance to get out of here with a little money in your pocket. Go see Brit. Sell for anything he'll give you. Otherwise, he'll close you out and you'll have nothing."

She was silent. He saw her face harden, saw the red spots in her cheeks.

"I'm remembering you saved my life this morning, Peg," he said. "I'd like to do more for you, but I can't. You'll have to leave the valley."

Dunning's and Heinz's bodies had been removed from the street, but men still stood in little groups, talking. Peg turned from the window and looked at Kim, her face softening.

"Why do you want to help me?" she asked.

"I told you," he answered. "You saved my life."

"That all?"

There was more, much more, but he had no words to tell her about this fault of his, this loyalty to the Clawhammer that had been as misplaced as her faith in Dutch Heinz had been. But if she stayed, there would be more trouble. There had been enough.

"That's all," he said. "You haven't got a friend in the valley but Limpy. He said to tell you he'll go with you."

"Not a friend in the valley," she said, as if talking to herself. "I'm Sam Cody's girl. I guess that's the whole trouble. He never tried to make friends. I have, but now there's just Limpy." She put her hands behind her back, fingers laced together, eyes on his lean face. "You've been right about a lot of things, Kim, and I've been wrong. I guess you're right about this. I'll see Bonham and I'll ride out of the valley with Limpy."

If she felt any grief over the deaths of Dunning and Heinz, she gave no indication of it. She moved past him and out of the hotel, her shoulders square, her face rigid, hiding all emotion.

Kim could not hate her, even when he thought of Yuma Bill. She had gambled everything, utterly ignoring all rules, and now she had lost everything that was important to her. She was not escaping her punishment. She would never be free from the torment of her thoughts, the regret that came from failure.

Kim waited until Peg disappeared into the bank, then he walked to the drug store. Doc Frazee stood in front with Luke Haines and Fred Galt.

"There's some men at the Clawhammer who need you, Doc," Kim said.

"I'll go out right away," Frazee said.

"Peg will be out for her things. Tell Fawcett and the rest of 'em she's leaving the valley."

Frazee cleared his throat. "I've been waiting to talk to you, Kim. Maybe you heard that Ed Lane lit a shuck. How would you like the sheriff star?"

"I never packed a star in my life."

"We ain't worried about how you'll make out," Frazee said quickly, and even Fred Galt nodded agreement. "We need a good man, now that we've got a new deal for the valley."

"Let me think about it, Doc," Kim said. "Right now I've got a ride to make."

Frazee grinned. "Sure. And Shorty's goin' to be all right. He came around before I left Fawcett's."

Kim strode to his horse and mounted, glad to hear that Shorty Avis would make it. He rode out of town filled with a driving urgency to see

Rocky, and his thoughts were all of what he wanted to say to her.

Hours later he reached the Fawcett place. The door was open and he saw Rocky's slim figure in the rectangle of light. Promptly he forgot every word he had planned to say to her.

She ran to him, crying—"Kim, Kim!"—and he came down off his horse in a quick, swinging motion and opened his arms to her. She was in them then, saying again—"Kim, Kim!"—and he found her hungry lips.

It was like no other kiss had ever been, and he knew now what Yuma Bill had meant when he had said there were some things that lasted and a man had to find them for himself.

She drew back, and looked up at him, her hands cupped against his cheeks, and he remembered then some of the things he had planned to say. "I love you," he said. "I never knew what love was before, but I've learned from you."

"I know how I felt about you," she said simply, "and I kept hoping that sometime you'd feel the same way about me."

"But I was twins. You were loving the man you wanted me to be."

She laughed softly. "I was loving the man you were, the real Kim Logan. You just had to find out for yourself. When you came back, I knew you'd found out."

"I reckon you'd call that faith," he said. "You

were right about something else, too. About me being a snake stomper and not a brush popper. I kept telling myself I wanted a ranch, but seems like it's kind of hard to get away from stomping snakes. They asked me to be sheriff, but if you . . ."

"It's what you want, isn't it, Kim?"

"Yes, but . . ."

"Then it's what I want."

He held her close, loving her and wanting her to know it. His drifting years were behind him, the years that had belonged to the old fiddle-footed Kim Logan who Brit Bonham had not entirely trusted, a Kim Logan who had known only the transient values of life. The past was a turned page; the future was a clean white one ready to be written upon. They would write upon it together, Kim Logan and Rocky Avis.

About the Author

Wayne D. Overholser won three Spur Awards from the Western Writers of America and has a long list of fine Western titles to his credit. He was born in Pomeroy, Washington, and attended the University of Montana, University of Oregon, and the University of Southern California before becoming a public schoolteacher and principal in various Oregon communities. He began writing for Western pulp magazines in 1936 and within a couple of years was a regular contributor to Street & Smith's *Western Story Magazine* and Fiction House's *Lariat Story Magazine*. *Buckaroo's Code* (1947) was his first Western novel and remains one of his best. In the 1950s and 1960s, having retired from academic work to concentrate on writing, he would publish as many as four books a year under his own name or a pseudonym, most prominently as Joseph Wayne. *The Violent Land* (1954), *The Lone Deputy* (1957), *The Bitter Night* (1961), and *Riders of the Sundowns* (1997) are among the finest of the Overholser titles. *The Sweet and Bitter Land* (1950), *Bunch Grass* (1955), and *Land of Promises* (1962) are among the best Joseph Wayne titles, and *Law Man* (1953) is a most rewarding novel under the Lee Leighton pseudonym. Overholser's Western novels, whatever the byline, are based on a solid knowledge of the history and customs of the 19th-Century West, particularly when set in his two favorite Western states, Oregon and Colorado. Many of his novels are first-person narratives, a technique that tends to bring an added dimension of vividness to the frontier experiences of his narrators and frequently, as in *Cast a Long Shadow* (1957), the female characters one encounters are among the most memorable. He wrote his numerous novels with a consistent skill and an uncommon sensitivity to the depths of human character. Almost invariably, his stories weave a spell of their own with their scenes and images of social and economic forces often in conflict and the diverse ways of life and personalities that made the American Western frontier so unique a time and place in human history.

Center Point Large Print
600 Brooks Road / PO Box 1
Thorndike, ME 04986-0001 USA

(207) 568-3717

US & Canada:
1 800 929-9108
www.centerpointlargeprint.com